When Kate started her nursing career at Northleigh Hospital, she was thrilled to recognise the consultant surgeon as a long-time friend of her brother's. Might her childish hero-worship now blossom into something more mature? Or was she looking in the wrong direction altogether?

FIRST YEAR LOVE

BY
CLARE LAVENHAM

MILLS & BOON LIMITED
London · Sydney · Toronto

First published in Great Britain 1980
by Mills & Boon Limited, 15–16 Brook's Mews,
London W1

© Clare Lavenham 1980

Australian copyright 1980
Philippine copyright 1980

ISBN 0 263 73406 4

Set in 11 on 13½ pt Times

*Made and printed in Great Britain by
Richard Clay (The Chaucer Press) Ltd.,
Bungay, Suffolk*

CHAPTER ONE

I HAD unpacked my clothes and put them tidily away. My family photographs were dotted about the room and should have made it seem more homely, but somehow they weren't succeeding very well.

There was nothing wrong with the room itself; it had all that was needed for sleeping and studying. But it was all terribly basic, and I was used to the cheerful clutter of the lovely old house by the river at Glendale where I'd lived for nearly nineteen years with my parents and brothers and an assortment of dogs and cats.

'I expect you'll be a bit homesick in London at first, Kate,' my mother had warned me. 'You've never been away before, except for holidays, and you're such a country girl.'

I'd laughed at her—actually *laughed*! And now here I was, sitting on the edge of my bed and absolutely wallowing in home-sickness.

It hadn't been like this six weeks ago when I started my preliminary training at Northleigh Nurse Education Centre. I'd thoroughly enjoyed the schoolgirl atmosphere, sudden friendships and absence of strain. Learning to be a nurse had been fun then, with a life-size doll as patient, and oranges to stick hypodermic needles in.

But that was all over now. In future nursing would be for real and, in addition to my home-sickness, I was quivering with nerves as I imagined all the mistakes I was certainly going to make.

Luckily a tap on the door forced me to get a grip on myself. I called out 'Come in' and Prunella Hunt appeared. We had shared a room at the old-fashioned training centre, and I was pleased to find we were next to each other now that we had moved to the Nurses' Home at the hospital.

'Have you finished, then?' Prunella glanced round at my few possessions and raised her fine dark brows slightly.

I answered her expression rather than her actual words. 'I didn't bring much from home—I hate travelling with a lot of luggage.'

'Come and see my room. I've tarted it up so the Warden would hardly recognise it.'

I followed her along the corridor and halted in the doorway with a gasp. The walls were decorated with posters stuck on with Blu-Tack, and the arm-chair and the bed were heaped with gaily-coloured cushions. A reading lamp in an elegant shade glowed softly at the desk, replacing the angled lamp provided by the hospital. Expensive and exotic-looking ornaments occupied every available surface.

'Like it?' Prunella asked.

'It's super! Do you think you'll be allowed to get away with it?'

'Most of it, I hope.' She frowned, staring about her with a critical air. 'Perhaps I have overdone it a bit, but I came by car and I could have brought the kitchen sink as well if I'd wanted to.'

Prunella lived at Richmond, with her mother and step-father. She didn't seem to get on with either of them and to hear her talk you'd imagine she'd only taken up nursing to get away from home. We were completely different and yet we got on well together, and I hoped it would continue that way.

'Take some of my cushions,' she now suggested, thrusting three of them into my arms. 'They'll cheer your room up no end.'

She came with me to supervise the disposal of the cushions to get the best effect, and then we returned to her room and sat down to debate what we should do for the rest of the evening.

'It's no good asking me—I haven't a clue,' I said, staring out at the mixed-up London skyline and wondering whether the drone of traffic ever ceased.

There must have been something of my feelings in my voice for Prunella stared at me.

'You don't sound exactly in a rejoicing mood because we've arrived at last,' she accused me.

7

'What's up, Kate?'

I decided on partial frankness. 'I'm scared! I know for sure I shall make every mistake in the book and then invent some!'

'Of all the defeatist attitudes!'

'I'm not being defeatist. I just happen to know my limitations, added to which I've got an absolute dragon of a Sister who's already made it plain she can't stand first-year student nurses.'

We had both been appointed to surgical wards, Prunella to Nightingale—a women's ward—and I to Fleming, which accommodated about forty male patients. We had already spent odd afternoons in our wards, learning our way about and helping with simple jobs.

On one occasion I had managed to spill a cup of tea over a patient's bed, a terrible deed which had caused me to plumb the depths of utter shame.

'I hope you're not always as clumsy as this, Nurse Wilding,' Sister had said fiercely. 'There is no room for clumsiness in nursing.'

Sister Battle—known throughout the hospital as The Battleaxe—was one of the last of the old type of Sisters. Nearing retirement, she ruled her ward with absolute authority. House surgeons quailed before her and even registrars treated her with exaggerated respect.

'You mustn't let her see you're frightened of her,' Prunella was saying. 'She'll bully you if you do and you'll go on being scared.'

'It's easy to talk!' I protested. 'You've never even met The Battleaxe and your ward Sister seems to be completely different.'

'Sister Roberts is young and pretty and a real honey. She calls all her student nurses by their christian names.' She changed the subject. 'Shall we go to the cafeteria and get something to eat? That ought to use up a bit of time.'

We went down three flights of stairs and found a sort of tunnel which went to the main hospital block. We managed to locate the cafeteria and eventually loaded our trays with plates of salad.

When we looked round for a table we couldn't see a vacant one anywhere. The place was full of nurses, in and out of uniform, young doctors and medical students, for Northleigh was one of the big London teaching hospitals.

'Looks like we shall have to share——' I was beginning when two boys wearing faded jeans and sweaters started making violent signals that we should join them.

'I suppose we might as well,' Prunella said carelessly in an undertone. 'They don't look too bad.'

As we sat down they gazed at us with frank curiosity and the dark one—who had a beard and a lot of curly hair—said, 'You're new here, aren't you?'

We agreed that we were, and the fair boy, whose

hair was neatly cut and only just touched his collar, suggested we should introduce ourselves.

'I'm Jeremy Bradford,' he told us, 'and this slovenly type is Neil Mackintosh, but he's always called Mac.'

After we'd given our own names Prunella asked if they were students.

Mac drew himself up with dignity. 'We're *doctors*, I'd have you know. I'm a house physician and Jeremy is ditto surgeon. In the medical hierarchy we admit to being the lowest of the low, but we both have ambition and expect to climb high in our profession.'

'And the best of British luck!' Prunella laughed and picked up her knife and fork.

I could see that both boys were dazzled by her looks and I couldn't blame them. Prunella's long silky hair was jet black and she had blue eyes with dark lashes. Her skin had that marvellous translucence which gives a lovely natural colour, and her tall slender figure would have done fine for a model.

Beside her I couldn't hope to compete, but I didn't let it bother me. You can't grow up among boys and cherish any illusions about your looks. Shorter and plumper, with a round face and slightly upturned nose, I knew that my only good point was my hair, which was the sort of golden brown which has lighter streaks in it.

The conversation was tossed lightly backwards and forwards—with Prunella and Mac doing most of the talking—while we ate our salad, and then Jeremy suggested adjourning to a pub near the hospital.

'It's only just across the road and we can be bleeped if we're needed.' He touched his pocket where a small flat object could just be seen. 'Officially we're on call and not on duty, but the two states are often indistinguishable.'

Prunella agreed with the suggestion at once and I also accepted with enthusiasm. I was already feeling quite a lot better.

The pub had a Victorian decor and a blaring juke box; it was absolutely packed and very hot and noisy, and I couldn't help comparing it with the old stone-built village inn at home.

'What'll you have?' Mac's voice jerked me back to the present and I asked for a lime and lager.

Fortunately most people seemed to prefer standing at the bar and the four of us found a small table in a corner and squeezed round it. Prunella was talking gaily and Jeremy and Mac seemed to be hanging on her words.

After a while Jeremy seemed to realise I was still there and he turned to me with a question.

'Where are you from—er—Kate?'

I told him it was Glendale, an obscure village in North Yorkshire where my father was the local doctor.

'It's an absolutely super place,' I went on. 'There's the river and the moors, and you can ride or walk for miles and miles and never see a soul.'

Jeremy's thick fair brows lifted in a supercilious way, or so it seemed to me. 'If it's all that special, what on earth brought you to London to train? Surely there's a hospital much nearer the paradise you've been describing?'

'Yes, of course.' I was annoyed at his tone. 'But I more or less had to come to Northleigh because my mother was a nurse here and my father also trained at this hospital. They met and fell in love when she was a student nurse and he was a house-man.'

'How very romantic! I hope she finished her training?'

'She did, as a matter of fact.' I ploughed on with the family saga. 'Simon, my eldest brother, was at the Medical School here too, so when I decided I wanted to be a nurse there couldn't be any question of training anywhere else.'

'It would obviously be quite impossible to break with the family tradition,' Jeremy observed solemnly. 'If my arithmetic is correct, you're the fourth member to come to Northleigh?' He raised one eyebrow slightly and his blue-grey eyes studied me with—I was convinced—a cynical gleam. 'Will there be any more?'

'Not until we start on the next generation,' I told him. 'I'm the only girl and my other four brothers are all older than I am, and they've already chosen their professions.'

'You've got *five* brothers?' I had actually impressed him at last but his next words didn't please me. 'I bet that means you've either grown up thoroughly spoilt or exceedingly tough. Which is it?'

'I'm certainly not spoilt! I can play cricket and football and I know how to defend myself in a scrap. I suppose you could say I'm tough.'

'You might find that handy in the streets around here,' Jeremy said. 'It's a pretty rough neighbourhood and one of the Northleigh sisters got mugged walking from the tube station not long ago.'

If he'd intended to scare me he didn't succeed. My mother had told me I would be quite safe provided I always wore my hospital scarf. It was many years, of course, since she'd been a nurse here, but I thought it likely the local people still venerated Northleigh as being 'their' hospital.

The conversation switched to social events and the spotlight was off me. Having done his duty, Jeremy was now free to give Prunella his full attention again and I heard him telling her with some enthusiasm that there was a disco every Friday evening.

'You must come the first Friday you're free,' he

13

urged, and it was Mac who said kindly, 'You too, Kate, of course.'

We both said we'd like to go but we didn't know anything about our duty times yet, except that we had to report at seven forty-five in the morning.

'Which wards are you on?' Mac asked.

When we told him Nightingale and Fleming his face fell.

'I shan't be seeing you in the course of duty, I'm afraid. I'm house physician on the paediatric team. But Jeremy is in and out of both wards all day long—you'll undoubtedly get sick of the sight of him.'

I couldn't help wishing it could have been the other way round, though in my lowly position I knew I wouldn't have any contact—or not much—with the various teams. Just at that moment Jeremy's bleeper started up and he went dashing off while the rest of us, deciding it was time to go, followed more slowly.

Fresh cool air was blowing from the direction of the river, and the smell of exhaust which had choked my country-bred nostrils seemed much less obvious. As we crossed the main road I saw the great city stretching away in both directions, brilliantly lit and exciting. There was so much to see and so much to learn about, and the future beckoned with a promise of wonderful things to come.

At that moment I wouldn't have wanted to be anywhere else in the world, not even Glendale.

In the morning my fears returned with a rush. I was awake before the bell and easily found a vacant shower. Back in my room, I began to put on the clothes which I had laid ready the night before.

One thing which hadn't changed since my mother's time was the Northleigh uniform. The student nurses wore brown-and-white stripes in heavy cotton material, and the dresses were calf-length and long-sleeved, with a prim white collar. The only difference was that Mum had worn black lisle stockings and I had black nylon tights.

I had a bit of trouble with my cap because my hair wouldn't lie flat, and just as I'd succeeded in anchoring it firmly Prunella came in.

She looked—naturally—superb in her uniform and with her hair in a sophisticated roll, but as we surveyed each other critically I was surprised to notice approval of my own appearance in her eyes.

'You look nice, Kate. I never realised what a tiny waist you have, and that fitting dress shows off your curves very well.'

'Don't talk about my curves!' I begged. 'Anyway, you've seen me in uniform before.'

'I never really *looked* at you.' She glanced at her watch. 'Come on—we ought to be on our way to

15

the dining room.'

'I don't think I want much breakfast,' I confessed as we set out. 'I've got só many butterflies in my stomach there isn't room for food.'

But Prunella said a good breakfast would banish the butterflies. I tried to believe her but it didn't work out that way, and by the time we parted and I continued on my way to Fleming Ward my fears of the night before had all returned to overwhelm me.

I approached the locker room nervously and found it full of nurses putting on their aprons and adjusting their caps. No one seemed to notice me except a red-haired girl who said with an air of enormous relief, 'Thank goodness you've come! Now I shan't be the most junior any more.'

'Is it a very uncomfortable position?' I asked. 'Do you get blamed for everything that goes wrong?'

'Not quite *everything*, but The Battleaxe doesn't like very junior nurses. You can understand it in a way; after all these years her patience is wearing thin.'

My apprehension was increasing rapidly. I fastened my own apron as quickly as possible and followed the red-haired girl—who said her name was Jean Sadler—into the ward.

Fleming looked very different at that early hour from how I remembered it on my previous visits.

No flowers, of course, and all the patients in bed. Some of the more helpless were being washed and I thought the night nurses looked dead on their feet.

When I reported to the Staff Nurse in charge she sent me off to help with bed-making. This should have been easy, but the nurse I was teamed with obviously found my careful slowness exceedingly trying. She gave a great sigh of relief when we finished and produced a weary smile.

'Don't worry—you'll soon speed up.'

As I hesitated, wondering what to do next, she told me to go round the ward and make sure all the patients had their bed tables in position for breakfast.

The design of Fleming Ward was very up-to-date, with a wide central corridor where there was a sort of reception desk. All around glass panels shut off small four-bedded rooms, and there was also a comfortable day room where meals were served for 'up' patients. Some of the men looked so ill I didn't dare to speak to them, but others greeted me cheerfully and welcomed me to the ward.

I was almost beginning to feel at home when Sister came on duty and summoned me to her office.

She was a small square woman with brown eyes and a penetrating stare. The dark blue dress which made the younger sisters look so glamorous did nothing for her sallow skin, and the beautiful elaborately pleated cap looked incongruous perched on very short iron-grey hair.

'Good morning, Nurse Wilding,' she said crisply, looking me up and down and apparently finding nothing amiss. She went on to give me a brief pep talk all about the high standard expected from Northleigh nurses, and then ended by reminding me that the patient's welfare must always come first.

It was corny stuff and I'd heard it all before, and yet it had the effect of making me suddenly tremendously proud to wear the Northleigh uniform. I went off to help serve breakfast full of good resolutions.

When the time came to gather round Sister for the report on each patient I tried hard to memorise every name and operation and the present state of each man's health. It was impossible, of course. By the time she reached the last few I'd forgotten all the earlier ones.

My next job was a pleasant one. I was told to bring in the flowers, and this again brought me into contact with the patients.

I had just put down a vase of yellow chrysanthemums on somebody's locker when the patient—a middle-aged man with tubes attached to him—said hoarsely, 'Do me a favour, love. Fetch me a glass of water; I'm that dry you'd think I'd swallowed the Sahara.'

'Yes, of course.' I sped away to the kitchen, found a glass and filled it to the brim.

Carrying it with great care, mindful of the spilt cup of tea, I made my way back towards the thirsty patient. I was just approaching his bed when I heard a quiet voice behind me.

'Where are you taking that water, Nurse?'

I spun round and found Jeremy standing in the doorway with a strange expression on his face, a mixture of anxiety and exasperation.

I said innocently, 'To Mr Walker. He asked me——'

'I daresay he did. He was taking advantage of your being new to the ward but——'

He broke off and to my horror, I saw that Sister had joined him in the doorway. She took in the situation at a glance.

'Go right up to the bed, Nurse Wilding,' she snapped, 'and read what it says on that white card—that is, if you *can* read. Then come to the desk and speak to me.'

I turned so quickly that the water slopped down my apron. As I raised my eyes to the notice I saw written in capital letters: NIL BY MOUTH.

The other three patients in the room were all staring at me with interest and Mr Walker made a rueful grimace and closed one of his eyes in a

19

wink.

'It was worth a try, love. Sorry you've got into trouble.'

'It's—it's all right.' I turned and fled, brushing past Jeremy without looking at him and spilling even more of the water.

Sister was writing something on a form. She kept me waiting nearly a minute and then looked up.

'Well, Nurse? What have you got to say for yourself?'

'I'm—I'm sorry, Sister. I hadn't seen the notice.'

'But it was your duty to have seen it. Do you realise that if the patient had tried to drink that water it would have done him serious harm? Notices of that sort are not put up for amusement, you know.'

She went on and on and I felt smaller and smaller. Jeremy went past and I sensed that he had glanced at me, but I kept my eyes fixed on the floor at my feet. I was almost in tears by the time Sister had finished.

It was over at last and I was dismissed to put on a clean apron. By the time I returned to the ward I knew that all my confidence had gone; I was once more the scared newcomer, petrified of doing the wrong thing.

During my absence a medical team had arrived to start the round. Two youngish men in long white coats I knew to be registrars, and there were also two in short white jackets—one of whom was Jeremy—and four or five students. They seemed to have mislaid the consultant who should have been leading them, and they hung around in a corner, talking among themselves.

He came in quietly as I stood hesitating, wondering what I was supposed to be doing, and automatically I turned to look at him, a tall young man—quite extraordinarily young—with dark slightly wavy hair, cool grey eyes and a lean face with strong features.

I stared at him incredulously and then forgot where I was, the trouble I'd just got into with Sister, the necessity for conducting myself with extreme care and everything else. I flung myself towards the newcomer and grabbed him by the arms.

'Nick! How absolutely wonderful to see you! But what *on earth* are you doing here?'

CHAPTER TWO

NICK MARSTON looked down at me in astonishment and then grinned. 'Good God—it's Podge!'

'For goodness' sake don't call me that here! Nobody's ever heard that old name at Northleigh, and it doesn't fit any more.'

'It certainly doesn't.' His smiling gaze scanned me briefly. 'You *have* grown up, Kate, and it's great to see you again, but I hardly think this is quite the time or place for a grand reunion.' He lowered his voice. 'Give me a ring some time and we'll fix something up.'

It most certainly was *not* either the time or the place. Glancing round belatedly I registered the astonished gaze of three student nurses and the scandalised face of a Staff Nurse. Sister came briskly out of her office.

To my amazement she ignored me completely and gave her attention to Nick.

'Good morning, Mr Marston. Your team is waiting for you.'

They went off to join the others. I slunk into a corner and wished the beautifully polished floor would open and swallow me.

Staff Nurse Denman approached me purposefully. 'You really will have to watch it, Nurse. Junior student nurses do not—repeat *not*—rush up to consultants and practically embrace them in the ward. What on earth came over you?'

I was delighted at her more-in-sorrow-than-in-anger attitude and did my best to explain.

'I was so surprised and pleased I didn't stop to think. Nick Marston is a friend of my eldest brother and I've known him for years and years, but since he got married we seem to have lost touch. I had no idea he was a consultant at North-leigh.'

'He hasn't been one for long,' she told me, 'and he's certainly very young. They say he's got a brilliant future in front of him.'

'He was always very clever,' I agreed, 'and hell-bent on surgery right from the start, whereas my brother is an ordinary G.P. and in partnership with my father.'

'Fascinating as your family history is, Nurse, I'm afraid we shall have to cut it short as I can see another team approaching.'

Staff Nurse Denman gave me a smile which sugared the acidity of her words and went to tell Sister that a silver-haired consultant, obviously much senior to Nick, was arriving. Sister came out and joined him, and the Staff Nurse took her place with Nick's lot.

'It's time for us to have our mid-morning break,' said a voice behind me, and Jean Sadler led the way to the locker room.

As we took off our aprons, she looked at me curiously. 'Do you always act as impulsively as you did just now, Kate?'

I gave the question my full consideration. 'Not *quite* always, but perhaps far too often. Why?'

'I don't think you realise what a crime you've committed. First-year nurses don't even *speak* to consultants.'

'But Nick's an old friend,' I interrupted.

'Not in the ward he isn't, and you'd better remember that or your life won't be worth living with Sister.'

'I'm already in her bad books,' I groaned. 'I expect she'll have me on the carpet again when the medical rounds are over.'

But, strangely enough, Sister didn't. She never even mentioned my regrettable behaviour and I assumed it was because she knew Staff Nurse Denman had dealt with me.

Another thing that surprised me was an alteration in the attitude of the other nurses. In some subtle way my prestige had gone up because of my friendship with Mr Marston, in spite of my idiocy in proclaiming it like that. It was all rather puzzling because I simply couldn't think of Nick as a person of so much importance.

I had adored him when I was in my early teens. He'd been like an extra brother—not that I needed any more—only much nicer because he never beat me up or stole my diary, or did any of the horrible thhings brothers do. He'd stayed at our house a lot and the nearest he'd ever come to annoying me was when he teased me about my plumpness.

During the afternoon I took advantage of Sister being off duty to ask the nice Staff Nurse if I could look up Nick's phone number in the office.

'I suppose so, since he's such an old friend.' She looked amused.

I scribbled it down on the underneath corner of my apron, the way I'd seen other nurses making notes of things they wanted to remember, and I made up my mind to get in touch that evening if possible.

Prunella and I were both off duty at five o'clock, since we'd worked through from early morning without much time off for meals. Collapsing with our feet up, we compared notes and I found that my day had been full of drama compared with hers.

'You actually know Mr Marston?' she exclaimed when I recounted my meeting with Nick. 'You've never mentioned him before.'

'I didn't know he was at Northleigh.'

'He did a round in our ward this morning,' Prunella went on. 'The Nightingale nurses all think he's very dishy and I don't believe Sister Roberts is entirely indifferent to his charms. Is he married?'

'Afraid so!' I laughed. 'But I've never met his wife, though I suppose I'm quite likely to now. He wants me to ring him so we can fix a meeting.'

Prunella seemed quite impressed and urged me to get on the phone without delay, but I pointed out Nick would be more likely to be at home if I waited until later.

I rang him at nine o'clock and was lucky enough

to have him answer in person.

His voice sounded exactly as it had always done and a little tremor of emotion went over me as I was swept back into the past.

'It's me—Kate,' I said a little breathlessly. 'You asked me to get in touch.'

He'd actually said 'Give me a ring some time' and I got the impression he was surprised I'd been in such a hurry, but his voice was cordial enough.

'You must come round to the flat and have a meal, Kate, so we can catch up on all the news. Goodness knows when I last heard from Simon, and I'm afraid I'm not much of a correspondent either.'

'That would be lovely,' I told him, meaning every word of it. 'When shall I come?'

The tiny pause at the other end of the line made me turn pink with mortification. He didn't really want to see me after all—he'd only been making a gesture. But when he spoke there was no hint of that in his friendly tones.

'I'm free on Friday evening. How about you?'

I had memorised my duties for the week and I answered promptly that Friday would be one of those days when I finished early.

'Good,' Nick said. 'Come round about eight o'clock. I think I can promise you a reasonable meal.'

What on earth did he mean by that? Was his

wife a doubtful sort of cook, someone who had good days and bad days? I puzzled over it but found no solution. I would have to wait until I met her.

'My flat's only about ten minutes walk from the hospital, overlooking the river.' He gave me the address. 'You should be able to find it quite easily. I shall look forward to seeing you.'

I replaced the receiver and went thoughtfully back to report to Prunella, who was lying flat on her bed in a state of exhaustion.

'He didn't ask you to bring a friend with you?' she enquired. 'No? Well, perhaps it's better not if you're going to talk about your family and Glendale all the time. I already know quite a lot about both.'

I remembered Jeremy's sarcasm regarding my family fixation and it occurred to me that perhaps I did tend to overdo it a bit, but when I asked Prunella about it she only laughed.

'You're lucky to have a family you actually want to talk about. I wouldn't dream of discussing mine; it would be of no interest either to me or anybody else.'

It seemed very sad to me that she should feel like that, although I'm sure it didn't trouble her in the slightest. For once I felt too lazy to bother about expressing my opinion and we relapsed into a weary silence.

In spite of an early night, getting up in the morning was much more of an effort than the previous one had been. My legs still ached and my feet felt sore; I couldn't believe that these important parts of my anatomy would ever get used to such continual use.

In the ward I managed to keep out of Sister's way as far as possible and the morning was fairly peaceful. I was given some interesting jobs to do, like taking out stitches and helping with dressings, and I also gave injections and an enema.

It was Nick's operating day so we didn't see anything of him, and later in the day we had several of his cases in a semi-comatose condition.

I was put in charge of one of these, an elderly man who appeared to be still deeply unconscious, though I was told he was only sleeping off the effects of the anaesthetic. Bursting with importance and utterly absorbed, I stood by the bedside with my fingers on the pulse and my eyes on my watch. Suddenly a voice behind me made me jump.

'You look very efficient, Kate. I'm almost afraid to interrupt.'

I whirled round and found Jeremy grinning at me, his blue-grey eyes alight with amusement.

'Do you mind!' I said crossly. 'I've got to start counting all over again now.'

'Hang on a minute before you start or my dynamic presence may make you lose it a second time.'

I gave him a withering look but it slid off his thick hide unnoticed. He glanced over his shoulder and then went on speaking in a rapid undertone.

'Have you and Prunella checked your duty times yet? Mac and I are hoping to get to the disco this Friday and we'd like it if you'd come with us.'

I knew he really meant they'd like it if Prunella went with them and I was immensely pleased to be able to tell him I wouldn't be able to go.

'I've already got a date for Friday, thanks,' I said airily.

I looked straight at Jeremy as I spoke and I caught a look of surprise and some other emotion I couldn't give a name to, but all he said was, 'Already? You must be a fast worker.'

'Not at all. He's an old friend.' I turned my back and again applied myself to my task.

I thought he'd go away then but instead his voice came again. '*Another* old friend? Or is it possible you've got a date with the boss?' He was obviously remembering the way I'd greeted Nick.

'I can't see it's got anything to do with you, but as a matter of fact I *am* going to see Nick. He's invited me to dinner.' And, though it wasn't in the least necessary, I found myself telling him about Nick's friendship with my brother.

'That family of yours crops up all over the place,' Jeremy commented. 'Must be quite useful to have the sort of background that gets you dinner invitations from a consultant.'

I ignored that and he walked round to the other side of the bed.

'The patient's doing fine, Kate. No need to worry.'

'I'm not worrying,' I snapped. 'Just making a routine check, that's all.'

My pleasure in the task was giving way to irritation and it was all Jeremy's fault. I glared at him and for the third time took hold of the limp wrist. As I started counting, he shrugged his shoulders and sauntered away.

After that I tried to keep out of his way and, as I was still avoiding Sister if possible, my life in the ward became quite complicated. The days passed slowly but Friday came at last and my eager anticipation of the evening increased enormously.

Prunella tapped on the door just after I'd returned from a long hot soak in the bath and asked me if I'd like to borrow any of her make-up.

'I've noticed you use hardly anything, Kate. It doesn't matter in the ordinary way, but for a special occasion you ought to take a bit more trouble.'

I was inclined to agree with her. 'But I don't think I'd better tonight,' I said doubtfully, 'because I'm not much good at it. I don't want to arrive looking all smudgy.'

She laughed and told me I was absolutely right. 'Looking smudgy *afterwards* is perfectly okay, but you must get there looking cool and sophisticated. I'll do your face for you if you like—which is an extremely noble offer considering I'd much rather be going to dinner with Nick Marston than to the disco with the boys.'

I accepted her offer gratefully, but when she'd finished I hardly knew myself. My cheeks were delicately flushed, the freckles on my nose had disappeared and my mouth was beautifully tinted. That much was fine, but my eyes looked most peculiar with a white line along the lids and lashes stiff with mascara.

Prunella was surveying her handiwork with great satisfaction. 'You look super, Kate. I shall have to give you some lessons.'

'I don't look like me.'

'Yes, you do, but it's a different Kate. The face which was right for striding about the moors isn't suitable for a candlelit dinner with an attractive man.'

'You're making it sound so romantic,' I protested. 'I think you've forgotten his wife will be there.'

I'd been in danger of overlooking that myself, I now realised, but I didn't confess it to Prunella.

'Perhaps she'll be out?' she suggested. 'You never know your luck.'

And when I reached the seventh floor of Nick's block of flats it really did seem as though his wife had gone out for the evening. He opened the door to me himself, looking absolutely gorgeous in clothes which were informal and yet very smart—a white silk shirt with a brilliant tie, dark red velvet jacket and black trousers.

He kissed me lightly on the cheek and began unwinding the striped hospital scarf which I had twisted round my neck, remembering Mum's warning about the dangerous streets round Northleigh.

'Why are you all wrapped up like this?' he asked. 'It's a warm evening for late September.'

I told him about my mother's instructions and he laughed. 'Things have changed since her time, and only the older people still look up to Northleigh nurses and regard them as something special. I shall drive you back.'

He opened a door opposite and took me into a large lounge with a dining table in an alcove. It was, as Prunella had predicted, softly candlelit. It was also laid for only two people.

'Sit down, Kate, and I'll get you a drink.' Nick crossed to a side table. 'What's your favourite these days? It used to be coke, I remember.'

I couldn't possibly tell him I still liked coke and so I chose gin-and-tonic. We sat side by side on the settee, facing the electric fire, and sipped our drinks.

Suddenly Nick leaned forward and stared at me. 'You look different. Is it because you've grown up?'

'Partly.' I told him about Prunella making up my face for me. 'Do you like it?' I finished anxiously.

'Yes and no. It's very attractive but you're not the Kate I used to know so well—at least, not superficially.'

'You could hardly expect me to be,' I pointed out. 'I was only about fifteen the last time we met and I'm nearly nineteen now.'

'It's a long time.' Nick sighed and I sensed a change in his mood. 'A great deal has happened.'

'Not much has happened to me. Only passing exams and getting accepted for Northleigh. I suppose you could say leaving home was the first real event in my whole life.' The alcohol was making me talkative and I went on to describe the agonies of homesickness I'd suffered that first evening.

'Poor Kate.' Nick touched my hand briefly. 'Are you over it now?'

'Oh yes, thanks. I'm fine.'

He began to question me about my parents and brothers, asking how Simon was making out in general practice and whether the others were doing well. He poured me another drink without asking if I wanted it and I began to feel most peculiar. I was glad when he said we'd better eat or the food would be spoiled.

There was pâté for starters, followed by turkey slices cooked in wine and lots of other things, and finishing with ice cream and fresh peaches. Nick served the meal quickly and deftly, and I congratulated him on his skill.

I was getting more and more curious about the absence of his wife. He hadn't even mentioned her and I now saw a chance of introducing the subject in a roundabout way.

'You surely didn't cook all this delicious food yourself?' I asked.

'Yes, I did, Kate—except the pâté, of course. I'm getting quite handy in the kitchen.' He looked down at his plate, his lashes making dark shadows on his thin face in the candlelight. Two lines on either side of his mouth were deeply etched and I remembered they hadn't been there in the old days.

'I don't understand, Nick. You *are* married, aren't you?'

'At this moment in time—yes. But in a few months I shall be divorced, if it goes through okay, and there's no reason why it shouldn't.'

'Oh, I *am* sorry!' Impulsively I stretched my hand across the table and laid it on his. 'Are you very unhappy?'

He took my hand and held it tightly. 'Some-

34

times. But things went wrong right from the start; I've had time to get used to the idea of an unsuccessful marriage. Elaine and I were very much in love physically, but that sort of thing can't survive total incompatibility. She couldn't stand my job and the irregular and long hours I worked.'

'She must have known it would be like that when she married you,' I protested.

'Knowing it is one thing and actually having to put up with it is quite another.'

I was impressed that Nick should stand up for his wife after she'd let him down so badly and I said so, but he shrugged it off.

'She wasn't a girl with a lot of imagination—she couldn't help her reaction.' He bent his head and kissed my fingers. 'You're a sweet child, Kate, to be so sympathetic.'

'I'm not a child.'

'No, you're not.' He returned my hand to my side of the table and got up abruptly. 'I'll make some coffee.'

Afterwards I helped him wash up in the tiny kitchen. I wished there was more I could do for him, like ironing a shirt or sewing on buttons.

We sat down again by the fire and after a moment Nick moved closer and put his arm round my shoulders. My heart started racing like crazy and I felt so uptight I thought he must notice, but he didn't seem to.

After a while he started talking about Glendale again and gradually I relaxed. My head sank onto his shoulder and I felt the slight pressure of his cheek against my hair. I was so happy I could hardly bear it and I wanted to stay there like that for ever.

Suddenly, in the distance, I heard a clock striking a half-hour and Nick roused himself.

'Eleven-thirty. Time to take you back, love. You've got a late pass, I hope?'

'Oh yes.' I sat up reluctantly. 'I've had such a lovely evening, Nick, and it was wonderful to be able to talk about home. Everybody at Northleigh is already tired of the subject.'

'You must come again.' He had fetched my coat and scarf and I put them on reluctantly.

Nick picked up the two ends of the long scarf and playfully pulled on them to tighten it. I looked up into his face and gave a small gasp of protest.

He hesitated, and then with a swift movement he bent down and kissed me on the lips.

CHAPTER THREE

ON Saturday I was free in the morning and could have a long lie-in. It was a glorious feeling to hear the rising bell and know I could remain where I was, deliciously warm and lazy. I lay for hours in a semi-trance, half sleep, half waking, and letting my imagination dwell lovingly on the events of the previous evening.

All too soon it was time to get up and get ready for duty. When I was dressed I went along to the dining room for lunch.

Prunella was there, sharing a table with two other nurses. Luckily they soon departed and she immediately demanded, 'Well? How did it go?'

I found myself torn between a longing to pour out the full story of my visit to Nick's flat and a most unusual desire to keep it private. So I compromised and said sedately, 'I enjoyed it very much, thank you.'

'I should have been surprised if you hadn't.' Prunella looked down her nose at me. 'Unless, of course, his wife didn't make you feel welcome?'

That put me in a spot and I was obliged to admit that Nick's wife hadn't been there.

'Really?' Her curiosity immediately doubled. 'That's very interesting, specially as the grapevine says they don't get on. So it was just you and him?'

'Yes.' I took refuge in culinary details. 'The dinner was super. I made an absolute pig of myself.'

'I'm not in the least concerned with your disgusting greed,' Prunella said loftily. 'What I want to know is did he take advantage of his wife's absence to make a pass at you?'

Could that kiss be described as 'a pass'? I didn't know and I didn't care, and I certainly had no intention of telling her about it.

'Of course not. We spent the whole time talking about people we both know, and things that happened in the past when I was a school kid.' I warmed to my subject. 'Nick was a terrible tease in those days—you never knew whether to believe him or not. Once he told me he'd seen a ghost in the churchyard and I daren't go near the place after dark for months.'

'As far as I can make out, you seem to have wasted your opportunities.' She looked at me scornfully.

I didn't take her up on that and, as it was time for us to separate, she couldn't continue the catechism.

As soon as I reached Fleming Ward I sensed a difference in the atmosphere. Nurses were looking grave, and Sister, who at this time was generally getting ready to go off duty for the afternoon, was behind drawn curtains in one of the rooms.

'What's happening?' I asked Jean when we met in the sluice.

'There's an awful flap on,' she told me importantly. 'That perforated ulcer case suddenly started haemorrhaging like crazy and we had to rush about getting a transfusion fixed up.'

'He's okay now?' I interrupted anxiously. I knew the case she meant. Mr Johnson was a nice man whom we all liked.

'Well——' Jean sounded very doubtful. 'He's certainly better but they're still worried about him. His heart's playing up, you see. He's got a history of angina.'

That afternoon, as I went about my duties, I kept glancing at those drawn curtains. A patient was fighting for his life in there, with all the resources of Northleigh to help him.

'We shall have to wait and see,' Staff Nurse Denman told me when I ventured to question her. 'Mr Johnson won't be out of danger until tomorrow at the earliest.'

But we didn't have to wait that long. Sister stayed on duty all the afternoon and a senior nurse was always in attendance on the sick man. Mr Stewart—the consultant in charge of the case—came in and his registrars and housemen milled around in the ward constantly.

And yet, in spite of so much skilled attention, the patient died.

It happened just as I was thinking about my tea break. The nurse who'd been on special duty emerged suddenly and came to the open door of the room. Seeing me, she beckoned imperiously.

'Fetch Sister, *at once*!'

I scurried away to do her bidding, and for a little while there was increased activity.

It stopped as abruptly as it had begun, and before I had even guessed at the reason I was sent for to Sister's office.

'No doubt you are aware, Nurse Wilding, that we have had a death in the ward?' she asked quietly.

'I-I've been busy in the kitchen, Sister.'

'Well, you know now, anyway, and it was, of course, Mr Johnson.' She studied me thoughtfully. 'Death is not a very frequent occurrence, I'm glad to say, but it's something all nurses must come up against from time to time, no matter how young they may be. I don't know if you have experienced death in your own family?'

'N-no, I haven't—not yet,' I said nervously.

'It's better to meet it first when the deceased is a stranger,' she told me in quite a kindly way. 'I've therefore told the nurse who will be preparing the body for removal to the mortuary that you are to assist her. You will be expected to take charge of this task yourself before long, and it's not too soon to learn.'

We had, of course, been given some instruction in the Nurse Education Centre and we all knew we would have to be prepared to cope with death eventually.

My feelings were mixed as I followed a second

year nurse behind the curtains. I was proud because Sister had actually thought me mature enough for the experience, and terribly nervous in case I might not be able to take it.

'There's nothing to be afraid of,' I was told briskly. 'You'll soon get used to it. I don't mind so much with older people, but when it's a child— that I really do hate.'

'I don't think I could bear it.' I glanced apprehensively at the still figure.

'Oh yes, you could, if you had to. After all, it's only a very, very small part of nursing.'

Her matter-of-fact attitude helped me enormously. She talked all the time she was working, but whether it was for her own benefit or mine I had no means of telling. It wasn't until the job was done that I realised I was feeling a bit sick after all, and when I cleared away the washing things my hands trembled badly.

'Off you go for your tea break now, Nurse,' Staff Nurse Denman said.

Obediently I took off my apron and set out for the cafeteria. I'd only just reached the top of the first flight of stairs when I met Jeremy.

'You all right, Kate?' He paused and eyed me keenly. 'You're looking a bit peelie-wallie, as Mac would say.'

'What on earth's that?' I asked, temporarily diverted from the uneasy sensations inside.

41

'Scotch for saying "pale", I *think*. What's wrong, then?'

'Nothing except that——' And I told him about my experience.

Jeremy listened quietly. 'We're all sorry when someone dies, but it's no good being too soft-hearted about it. Death is something doctors and nurses just have to take in their stride.'

'So you think I ought to be hard-hearted?' I flashed.

There was nobody about just then and Jeremy moved closer and put his hands on my shoulders.

'You know I didn't mean that, Kate.' He gave me a gentle shake. 'I'm recommending you to try and grow an extra skin, that's all.'

He went on talking and gradually the tight knot in my stomach unwound. Unfortunately the minute I stopped feeling tensed up my eyes filled with tears.

'*Now* what's the matter?' Jeremy looked at me in exasperation. 'I've been doing my best to make you see things straight and all the thanks I get is the threat of an emotional scene. You can't cry here, my girl, and certainly not when you're talking to me. Buzz off now and get yourself a cup of tea.'

His brusqueness had the effect of making me pull myself together pronto. I said furiously, 'You needn't imagine I *want* to stand here with you!'

and went down the stairs like a streak.

When I told Prunella about my afternoon she was amazed.

'Your Sister Battleaxe must be a right sadist to make you do that so early. Our Sister Roberts doesn't let us have anything to do with death until our second year.'

'Sister Battle believes nurses should develop into mature adults as soon as possible,' I said loftily.

We lost another patient in Fleming about two weeks later, but this time it wasn't unexpected, and then—right out of the blue—there was a death in my own family. My mother rang up one evening to tell me that my grandmother, who lived in the next village, had died.

'It would be nice if you could come for the funeral, Kate,' she said wistfully when she'd broken the news. 'We'd all love to see you.'

'It seems ages since I left home,' I agreed. 'I'll have to think about it and see whether it could be arranged.'

The trouble was Glendale was such a long way away that I couldn't get there and back in one day by train, even if I could fix it to have the day of the funeral completely free. With all my heart I longed to be with my family on this sad occasion, but I couldn't see how it was to be managed.

'Why don't you ask Nick to drive you?' Prunella suggested. 'Maybe he'd like to go, since he's such a friend of the Wildings. I expect he knew your grandmother.'

I was horrified at the mere idea. 'I couldn't possibly ask him! Besides, I don't know if Sister would let me change my duty so as to get away for a whole day. Grandmothers' funerals have always been a sort of joke and she might think I was making it up.'

'You can only ask her,' Prunella said, dismissing the matter.

There didn't seem much point in that when I had no way of getting to Glendale, but I kept on thinking about it and suddenly a solution offered itself.

I was dashing back to my room to make the bed and get a clean apron, and I was taking a short cut across the car park instead of going by the tunnel. Turning a corner I collided with someone and discovered it was Nick.

He held me firmly by both arms, smiling down at me so affectionately that my heart turned right over.

'I thought nurses weren't supposed to run except in cases of fire or haemorrhage. Which is it?'

'Neither. I didn't think it mattered out-of-doors,' I told him breathlessly.

'Perhaps it doesn't.' He let his arms drop. 'I've hardly seen you since you came to the flat, Kate. Where have you been hiding?'

'I try to keep out of the way when you come to the ward in case I should forget myself and speak to you,' I explained, laughing up into his face.

'Wise girl! How are you getting on?'

'Okay, I *think*. I haven't had any more trouble with Sister.'

'Which speaks for itself.'

'Yes.' I suddenly remembered my other problem and hesitated, and Nick immediately asked me what was on my mind.

'You have the most give-away face I've ever seen, Kate, so out with it.'

I didn't need any more encouragement to plunge right in. 'I've had upsetting news from home. My grandmother died very suddenly. Do you remember her, Nick?'

'Of course I do. A marvellous old lady—wore slacks and rode a moped. I'm sorry she's dead.'

'She gave up the moped a few years ago and stayed at home more.' I thought guiltily of how long it was since I'd visited her and it seemed all the more important that I should get to the funeral. Once more I hesitated.

Nick had always had a gift for guessing people's thoughts. He said rapidly, 'If you've got problems about getting to Glendale for the funeral, Kate, I might be able to help. When is it?'

'Oh, Nick—could you?' I gazed up at him hopefully and immediately poured out the details.

'Everybody at home would love to see you again, specially Simon. We could do it easily in one day in your car.'

'Of course we could. There'd be bags of time.' He frowned, lost in thought for a moment, and then said cheerfully, 'I'll have to work it out and let you know. But you can depend on me to give you a lift home if it's at all possible.'

In the midst of my exuberant thanks I heard a clock striking and gave a gasp of horror. 'I've got to be back in less than five minutes! 'Bye for now, Nick. You'll put me out of my misery as soon as possible, won't you?'

In actual fact I didn't really doubt for a moment that he would fix it. Consultants, I assumed, could order their lives to suit themselves, and if Nick wanted a day off to compensate for the amount of overtime he worked, then he could surely arrange it.

I was so confident that I went to Sister on my return to the ward and asked if I could change my day off. She heard me to the end without interruption, her beady eyes fixed on my face, and then said curtly,

'With some people I should regard that as a very suspect story indeed, but I think you are telling me the truth, Nurse Wilding. If you can find a nurse to accommodate you I shall have no objection.'

I quickly arranged it with Jean Sadler and then tried to wait with as much patience as I could for

46

confirmation from Nick.

The funeral was on a Thursday. On the Tuesday evening Nick phoned me at the Nurses' Home.

'I'm terribly sorry, Kate, but I can't make it to Glendale after all. Something has cropped up——' Hearing my gasp of dismay, he went hurriedly on. 'But don't despair, I've given my houseman the job of driving you. He's got a day due to him and he might as well make himself useful, since he didn't seem to have made any other arrangements.'

'*Jeremy?*' I could hardly believe that Nick could do this to me, but he didn't know how much I disliked Jeremy—most of the time anyway. 'What did he say about it? I can't believe he wants to do it.'

'I asked it as a personal favour. He could hardly refuse his boss without adequate reason and he made no attempt to get out of it. Personally, I think he's hellish lucky to have a trip out of London in the company of an attractive girl.'

I said quickly, 'I doubt if he finds me all that attractive.'

'Nonsense! Jeremy's got an offhand manner and, I sometimes suspect, an outsize chip on his shoulder, but it doesn't mean a thing. He's a good lad at heart.'

I neither knew nor cared about the state of Jeremy's heart. I was desolated at the loss of my

47

long day in Nick's company, but there was nothing I could do about it. Remembering my manners, I thanked him for the trouble he'd taken and hung up.

The following day Jeremy waylaid me in the ward kitchen.

'We ought to make an early start in the morning, Kate. The boss lent me his map book and I've worked out the route, but I'm not sure how long it will take.'

'I can be ready any time you like.' I avoided looking at him. 'I'm sorry you've got landed with such a chore, but it wasn't my fault,' I added stiffly.

'I expect I shall survive—and I hope the car does too. You'd better make sure you've got a late pass.'

'Do you think there's any doubt about the car?' I asked in alarm.

'Well, it's a bit ancient and not used to such a long journey, but I reckon it'll keep going, given a bit of luck. Can you manage seven o'clock?'

I said I could and Jeremy went away, leaving me wondering if he'd been frightening me for his own amusement, or whether he was really worried about his car. I spent the rest of the day alternating between excitement at the thought of seeing my family again, and regret both because of the reason for my visit and the means of getting there.

Jeremy was outside the Nurses' Home with a shabby old banger punctually at seven a.m. He was in an early morning sort of mood with little to say, and we drove through London in almost total silence. The car seemed to go quite well, but the heater wasn't very efficient and soon the cold spread up from my feet to my brain, so that I was glad no conversation was expected of me.

Things were better when we reached the outskirts of the city. Sun dispersed the morning mist and I began to warm up a little. I stopped moaning to myself about my bad luck in not doing the trip in Nick's comfortable car and with his attractive company, and started to get excited about the journey's end.

At this point it occurred to me that Jeremy would be at a loose end when we reached Glendale. I could hardly avoid inviting him to my home for the day.

'I don't know if you've got any plans—' I began diffidently.

Jeremy glanced sideways at me. 'I've heard so much about the wonders of Glendale that I intend to go off exploring when we get there.'

'I'm sure my mother——'

'No, Kate.' His voice was very firm. 'I wouldn't dream of intruding on your family when you've got a funeral on your hands. Don't give it another thought.'

49

I was very glad not to, but now that we'd started talking I found I wanted to keep on and I asked him where his own home was.

'I haven't one,' Jeremy said curtly.

'No home at all?' I was appalled that anyone should be so alone. 'But you must have some relations!'

'Why must I?'

'Well——' I was at a loss. 'Everybody has—at least I've always thought so. I've got masses scattered all over the north of England.'

Jeremy didn't answer until we had overtaken a lorry, and then he said, 'And I suppose they're all absolutely charming people and you adore the whole lot of them?'

'No, I don't, then! Some of them are awful and it wouldn't bother me if I never saw them again. But the Glendale lot are different—and Gran was one of the best.'

'I suppose there'll be a great crowd at the funeral?'

'Oh yes—sure to be. Northern people are very clannish, you know.'

'So I've always heard, but they aren't alone in being clannish,' Jeremy told me. 'The East End of London was the same when I was a kid, though it's changed now. Tower blocks don't make for friendliness.'

I was interested to be given this brief glimpse of

his background. 'I didn't know you were a Londoner. Did you live near the hospital?'

'Not far away. I was born at Northleigh, as a matter of fact.'

Questions came tumbling into my mind and almost out of my mouth. What had happened to Jeremy's parents? Why did he say he hadn't a home? What kind of people were they? Nick had said he seemed to have a chip on his shoulder and there must be a reason for this. Perhaps I was on the track of it?

'I expect you feel the hospital is a sort of home,' I suggested. 'Were you at the Northleigh Medical School?'

'Yes, I was, but if you really imagine there is anything homelike about a hospital, Kate, you must have an even more sentimental outlook than I thought.'

I turned on him angrily. 'I'm not sentimental! Why do you always have to be so horrible just because I've got a happy home and I like my family?'

There was a silence and, stealing a glance at him, I saw Jeremy was looking absolutely astounded.

'Do you really think I'm horrible?' he asked blankly at last. 'I don't mean to be.'

'You certainly are, whether you mean it or not. On my very first evening you made sarcastic remarks when I talked about home.'

There was another pause before Jeremy said in a low voice, 'Could be I was envious.'

'Oh! I never thought of that—but then I didn't know you were so alone in the world.' My anger melted away like magic. 'I'm sorry—I wish I hadn't said anything about it now.'

'There's no need to be sorry. It doesn't matter in the slightest,' he said stiffly. 'And if you're going to start mothering me it'll be even more unpopular than your constant references to your good fortune.'

All my sympathy for his apparently forlorn state was strangled at birth. 'You don't have to worry,' I flung back at him. 'I have absolutely no maternal feelings towards you, and I can't imagine any circumstances in which I would be likely to have any.'

Jeremy made a noisy gear change which I hoped meant I'd rattled him a bit. I sat staring straight ahead for at least five miles and suddenly realised he was laughing.

'What's so funny?' I asked coldly.

'Us. We're a couple of idiots wasting what's practically a day's holiday by scrapping and trying to score each other off. Let's call a truce, shall we? Just for today?'

'Suits me.'

I doubt if I could have kept up my annoyance

much longer in any case, with every mile bringing us nearer the wild countryside I loved. Already we had left the flat land behind us and low hills were appearing in the distance. The car was still going like a bomb and we ought to reach Glendale in good time for lunch.

Some time after entering Yorkshire we left the main road and turned into a network of less frequented roads. Jeremy seemed to have learnt the route by heart and he drove confidently until the last few miles.

'You'll have to navigate now, Kate,' he told me.

I was only too willing. Sitting bolt upright I directed him up a steep narrow hill with a hairpin bend at the top, down the other side and eventually out into a green valley with a small river gurgling swiftly over its stony bed.

'This is Glendale—we're here!' Excitement throbbed in my voice. 'And that's our house over there, the white one standing by itself.'

'I'll just drop you off and make tracks for the pub,' Jeremy said.

Suddenly I couldn't believe that, about one hundred and fifty miles back, I'd actually wanted him to go off alone.

'My mother will have a fit if I let you disappear. You must come and eat with us. There's sure to be plenty; besides, they were expecting Nick.'

'Then I'm afraid they'd find me something of a

disappointment. No, thanks, Kate. I'll put you down like I said, and then call for you again around five o'clock. Okay?'

I made another attempt to persuade him but he was adamant. And then I forgot all about him as I jumped out at the gate of Bridge House and went racing in to be received into the bosom of my family, while Jeremy continued on his solitary way to the inn.

CHAPTER FOUR

IT was over; the few hours with my family had passed in a flash. I had cried at the funeral and laughed at the tea-party afterwards, I had seen all my five brothers, three of their wives and several of my nephews and nieces. I had visited the old pony, been ecstatically greeted by the two dogs and played with the latest batch of kittens. Nothing remained to do now except wait for Jeremy to appear and collect me.

'I do wish he'd been willing to spend his time here,' my mother said. 'It seems so rude not to have given him any hospitality.'

'It was his own choice,' I reminded her.

'So you said, dear, but I wonder if you really tried hard enough to persuade him?'

'Of course I did, Mum.' I picked up the basket loaded with food which she'd prepared for me to take back. 'Jeremy's a bit of a loner—he might not have enjoyed being with such a big crowd and all strangers.'

'Perhaps it was for the best, then.' She pushed back the lock of curly grey hair which was always falling onto her forehead. 'The poor lad's probably shy. Did your father give you the money for the petrol? We mustn't let Jeremy be out of pocket.'

'Yes, he did.' I heard a car stop outside. 'Good-bye, Mum—I'll see you again before Christmas.'

They all came out into the front garden to see me off, and my parents—not unnaturally—insisted on being introduced. I could see they liked the look of Jeremy and I had to admit he was at his best, very polite and with just enough shyness to make my mother certain she'd been right about him.

At the last moment Simon, my eldest brother, came up and said, 'I understand you're Nick Marston's houseman, and I'd be obliged if you'd remind him we haven't seen him at Glendale for nearly three years, or heard from him either. We didn't even know he was a consultant until Kate told us. What on earth stopped him from coming today? Hadn't he got the nerve to face his old friends?'

'He—er—didn't give a reason.' To my surprise,

Jeremy seemed embarrassed but he rallied quickly and added, 'It must have been something quite unexpected and very important or I'm sure he would have taken the opportunity of coming to see you.'

'So I should hope.' Simon stepped back and I got into the car.

Everybody waved and I waved back until we turned a corner, and suddenly it was all terribly quiet and there was a huge lump in my throat which would have made it quite impossible for me to speak if Jeremy had said anything.

Fortunately he didn't, and we went on in silence for nearly fifteen minutes.

At last he said abruptly, 'What's all that, then?'

'In the basket? Food. Mum didn't want us to starve on the journey.' I suddenly remembered the fivers my father had thrust into my handbag. 'And Dad gave me the money for the petrol. I don't know how much it's costing, but I expect there's plenty.'

'There's no need for him to have done that.' Jeremy sounded startled. 'The boss said he'd make it right with me when he asked me to take his place. He's already given me a cheque and I'm to let him know if I want any more.'

'*Nick* paid? That was very generous of him!' I was touched at the gesture.

'To my way of thinking it was the least he could

do after letting you down.'

'He must have some very good reason.' I rushed to Nick's defence. 'Perhaps he was worried about a patient and didn't want to leave London.'

'There's nobody in either Fleming or Nightingale just now who couldn't be left,' Jeremy said flatly.

'Well, there's no need to keep on about it. You're making me feel you've got a grudge against Nick for letting you in for this long drive.' I waited a moment for him to deny it and then, since he remained silent, I finished a little anxiously, 'Perhaps you have?'

'For a girl who has a remarkably secure and happy background, Kate, you want a hell of a lot of reassuring!' His voice was full of exasperation. 'Have I really given you cause to imagine I've hated the trip?'

'N-no, not exactly, but——'

'But what?' Jeremy demanded.

'I'm never sure what you're thinking or how you're really feeling about anything.'

'My thoughts are my own affair,' he said fiercely, 'and my feelings too.'

'Okay.' I changed the subject. 'I had a terrible task trying to explain to my mother why you'd gone off on your own.'

'I'm sorry about that.' But he didn't sound sorry. 'And for your information, Kate, I had a great time at Glendale. After a ploughman's lunch at the pub I went for a walk on the moors which I very much enjoyed. Does that satisfy you?'

'Yes, thank you.'

Suddenly weary after so much emotion and such an early start to the day, I leaned back and relaxed. I think I probably slept for at least the next twenty miles.

When I woke up it was dusk and there was a lot of traffic, so I kept quiet and let Jeremy concentrate on driving. Soon it was quite dark and, as I fixed my eyes on the long beam of the headlights leading us back to London, I realised something.

Now that the distress of the actual parting had receded, I didn't mind returning to Northleigh in the slightest. This time I was most certainly *not* going to be homesick.

'Talk to me,' Jeremy ordered me suddenly. 'I'm getting sleepy.'

'I wish I could do some of the driving, but I never got around to taking lessons.' I glanced at his profile in the dim light and noticed for the first time that he had a very straight nose, well-shaped lips and a firm chin. 'What shall we talk about?'

'Glendale?' he suggested. 'That ought to keep you going until we reach London!'

I ignored the sarcasm and protested that he wouldn't want to listen to me burbling on about my home and family. 'You said you were—were envious. I don't want to make you feel worse.'

'Perhaps I'm a glutton for punishment.' He yawned openly. 'Anyway, for God's sake talk about *something*. I didn't get to bed until after midnight, and I was on call the night before, and it's all beginning to catch up with me.'

I snatched at the first thing which came into my head and described to him a sponsored walk over the moors I'd taken part in the previous autumn, and from that I went on to tell him what it was like to be snowed up in a moorland village.

'Once it lasted for nearly a week and we didn't have a freezer then and we were beginning to run out of food——'

But before I got to the end of my saga, Jeremy interrupted.

'Sorry, Kate, but I'll have to stop for a short break. It's dangerous to go on the way I feel at the moment.'

As he drew into a handy lay-by I remembered Mum had put in a flask of coffee, but when I offered it Jeremy said he'd have a nap first and then the coffee would be fine.

He switched off the engine and slid down in his seat, leaning his head back. Almost immediately he was asleep.

I wasn't in the least sleepy myself, but I kept very still and thought about the wonderful day I'd had—apart from the sadness over Gran—and how absolutely perfect it would have been if Nick had been able to come.

My dreams were brought to an abrupt end by the sudden pressure of a heavy weight on my shoulder. Jeremy's head had slipped sideways and come to rest against me. He gave a long sigh and settled himself more comfortably; he was obviously very deeply asleep.

On the way up to Yorkshire he'd warned me against attempting to mother him. But I couldn't help the wave of tenderness which swept over me as I braced myself to support him. He'd never know anything about it, anyway, nor that I let my cheek brush against the softness of his thick fair hair.

No doubt we'd be arguing again soon, or perhaps even quarrelling, but at that moment I didn't mind how long I had to sit there motionless if Jeremy was comfortable and had the rest he so badly needed.

Some time later he moved suddenly and turned his face towards my neck. His right arm came round and drew me closer; I felt the warmth and urgent pressure of his lips against my bare skin.

It wasn't tenderness I was feeling now but a violent and totally different emotion which gripped me with a force I found it impossible to resist. Moving instinctively, I bent my head, and Jeremy—still half asleep—raised his face to meet

60

mine. Our mouths met and clung, and I closed my eyes and gave myself to the astonishing sweetness of the moment.

I don't know how long the kiss lasted but Jeremy was the first to break away.

He said frantically, 'Good God, Kate—however long have I been asleep? Why didn't you wake me earlier?'

'I hadn't the heart—and you're not driving on until you've had some food and coffee.' I dived into the basket and began to drag out sandwiches and the flask. 'Another few minutes won't make much difference.'

'It might make all the difference between you being back by midnight, and getting locked out— or whatever it is they do.'

'You have to ring the bell and the night porter comes over from the main building, and then in the morning there's an awful fuss.' I paused in pouring coffee and looked at him in alarm. 'You don't really think there's any danger?'

He shrugged. 'It could happen, but with luck we should just make it. I hope so for your sake, Kate.'

'So do I.' I handed him a mug and poured one for myself. We drank as quickly as possible and ate two of the enormous sandwiches filled with York ham.

As soon as he'd finished Jeremy switched on and pressed the starter. Nothing happened except a half-hearted whirring.

'What's the matter? Why won't it start?' I sat bolt upright in alarm and poured out all the daft questions that car-ignorant people are apt to ask on that sort of occasion.

'How should I know?' Jeremy flung at me crossly. He got out and lifted the bonnet. 'There's a torch in the dash. Come and hold it for me, please.'

I groped on the shelf, full of dirty rags, an empty oil can, spanners and other odds and ends, and located the torch. As I stepped out a cold wind carrying flurries of rain snatched at me and sent my skirt up to my waist and my hair whirling round my head. Blinding headlights swept past uncaring as lorries and cars thundered on towards London.

Shivering, I switched on the torch and held it as directed by Jeremy.

'Looks like I'll have to clean the plugs,' he muttered.

'Will it take long?'

'Long enough to matter, perhaps, but it can't be helped. If only we hadn't stopped——'

'You needed that sleep,' I told him firmly.

How much did he remember of what had happened? Had he been more asleep than I'd realised? Or was he only pretending he didn't know anything about it because he bitterly regretted the whole astonishing episode? I would have given a great deal to know.

I debated the matter as Jeremy scratched away with a penknife at small sooty-looking objects. After what seemed an eternity, he replaced them under the bonnet and returned to try the starter. The engine fired at once.

'Sorry about that, Kate,' he said as we drove thankfully out of the lay-by.

'It wasn't your fault.'

'Yes, it was. I should have made time to clean the plugs before we left, even though they seemed okay.' He paused and then added bitterly, 'Nothing like that would have happened with Nick Marston's car—that's for sure.'

'He's a consultant,' I pointed out. 'He can afford to run a much more expensive car, but I expect you will one day—if you've got ambitions that way.'

'I'm not sure I want to stay in surgery. My first houseman job was with a medical team and I think I prefer it. In a way it's more of a challenge.'

'You get much more dramatic results with surgery,' I argued as we tore along the dual carriageway at a terrific speed.

'Who's looking for drama? Certainly not me. In fact, I sometimes think I would like to be a G.P.— if only I had any hope of raising the money to buy myself a share in a group practice.'

We went on talking about it until the far-flung tentacles of London caught us in their grip and the traffic thickened. It was already after eleven, but I felt reasonably sure we would make it in time.

Maybe we would have if we hadn't been held up by two lots of roadworks which hadn't been there in the morning.

'They'll work all night and try to get finished before the morning rush hour,' Jeremy explained as we waited in a long queue for the lights to change. 'But I wish they'd chosen some other night.'

I twisted my fingers together anxiously, my eyes alternately on the lights and a church clock which gleamed ominously above our heads. Twenty minutes to twelve. I had no idea how far we still had to drive but Jeremy's tenseness didn't reassure me. He let in the clutch with a jerk as we moved again at last, but we were obliged to crawl for a long way past flickering orange lights before we could overtake a lorry and get clear.

'There's no hope now, Kate,' Jeremy said after the second hold-up. 'You'll have to resign yourself to one hell of a row.'

'But surely they'll realise it wasn't our fault?' I turned to him in distress.

'Of course they won't. They'll say we should have started back sooner and allowed time for things to go wrong.'

We were passing St Paul's and the huge clock boomed out twelve strokes. Each one thudded down onto the top of my head and depressed still further the spirits I'd been struggling to keep up. They'd be locking the door at the Nurses' Home this very minute.

I pictured the Home Warden, a nice motherly woman with a no-nonsense look in her eye, checking the list of nurses who had permission to be out late. And finding only one of them not yet returned to the fold—me.

Neither of us spoke during the final part of the journey. At last Jeremy turned into the narrow side street in which the Nurses' Home stood and drew up before the massive door. Still in silence he sprang out and pressed the bell.

The wait seemed interminable but I remembered the porter would have a long way to come, and I didn't think he'd be likely to hurry himself either. I was just going to urge Jeremy to ring again when there came the sound of bolts being drawn back.

An elderly man in a brown coat looked out. 'What have you got to say for yourself?' was his greeting.

Jeremy took over and explained about the plugs. The man listened with a sceptical expression on his face and then motioned me inside.

'You'd better tell that to the boss in the morning, Nurse. Maybe she'll believe you and maybe she won't, but I don't rate your chances very high, specially as you were out with your boy-friend.'

'It happens to be the truth,' Jeremy said furiously.

'Oh yeah?' The porter grinned at us rather nastily.

'And he's not my boy-friend anyway,' I put in quickly.

'You could have fooled me!' His smile broadened. 'Sorry to tear you away, Nurse, but I don't want to stand here all night. Say goodbye quickly, there's a good girl, and let's get this door shut.'

I looked at Jeremy despairingly. I could see he was smouldering but he kept himself under control.

'Don't worry, Kate. It's going to be all right.'

I wished I could believe him.

I didn't sleep much that night and in the morning the Home Warden sent for me before I could escape to the dining room for breakfast. She listened gravely as I made my explanation and then told me she would have to report me to Miss Ferguson, the Senior Nursing Officer.

Speechless, I gazed at her in horror, and she went on talking in her quiet voice.

'You may think we're making a lot of fuss about your being late, Nurse Wilding, but I must remind you that Northleigh expects a very high standard of behaviour from its nurses. In the provinces, I believe'—she grimaced slightly in disgust—'the nurses come in more or less when they please at some hospitals. We shall never permit that sort of behaviour *here*, I sincerely hope.' Her tone softened slightly. 'Off you go now and have breakfast. Miss Ferguson will send for you when she can find time.'

I walked through the tunnel in a trance, totally unaware of the nurses who hurried past on both sides. Maybe this was the last time I'd ever walk along here, a Northleigh nurse in the uniform I loved and wore so proudly. The Warden hadn't even mentioned the possibility of my getting sacked, but it loomed so enormous in my mind that it blotted out everything else.

I couldn't eat anything except one piece of toast and Prunella exclaimed at my haunted look.

'What went wrong yesterday, Kate? Didn't you have a good day with your folks?'

'Super.' I paused to swallow uncomfortably. 'But I was late back and I'm in awful trouble.'

She listened sympathetically as I poured it all out, and then did her best to administer comfort.

'It wasn't your fault. It was just one of those things and might have happened to anybody.'

'I wish I could convince myself Miss Ferguson will see it that way,' I said gloomily.

Prunella ate the last fragments of her bacon and

put the knife and fork neatly together. 'Of course, it's a pity you were with a houseman. I'm afraid she's sure to take it for granted Jeremy's your boy-friend and you stopped in the lay-by for a session of necking.'

She was looking straight at me as she spoke and she couldn't miss the wave of hot colour which—to my fury—suddenly spread across my face.

'You *were* necking! But I thought you didn't like him, Kate? Did a whole day in his company make you change your mind?'

'I like him better than I did,' I admitted cautiously, 'and we weren't exactly necking. That is——'

My need to unburden myself that morning was beyond control. Within a few seconds I'd told Prunella all about Jeremy's surprising behaviour.

'And you don't call that necking!' she exclaimed when I'd finished. 'Well, some people have very high standards, of course.'

I let that pass because I badly wanted her opinion. 'The thing that's puzzling me is whether he was more asleep than I thought at the time. Maybe he even imagined I was someone else? We don't know anything about his private life.'

'A houseman doesn't have a private life, and I never heard Jeremy's name linked with anybody's. He must have known he was kissing *you*, but perhaps he regretted it afterwards and he wants you to think he didn't mean it.'

'Could be,' I said thoughtfully.

As I left the dining room I knew quite definitely that my conversation with Prunella hadn't cheered me up in the slightest.

When Sister came on duty she gave no sign that she knew of my crime, though I felt sure she must by now. The Sisters had a private dining room and the Warden would have told her. At report time it seemed to me that her eyes lingered on me disapprovingly, but perhaps that was due to my guilty conscience.

Time passed at its usual speed and suddenly I realised I was due to go for my break. We weren't supposed to leave the ward without permission, though I was tempted to this morning. As I dithered near the office, Sister looked out and called to me.

'Miss Ferguson has just phoned me regarding your late return last night. I must say I'm surprised and grieved you should have repaid my kindness in allowing you to change your day off in such a way.'

'The car broke down, Sister, and——'

She held up her hand and continued to eye me grimly. 'It is the Senior Nursing Officer you must give your explanation to, Nurse, but unfortunately it's impossible for her to see you today. She is fully booked this morning and has interviews with would-be nurses all the afternoon. She will try and fit you in tomorrow.'

I didn't know whether to be glad or sorry about my temporary reprieve, and I was debating the subject and not looking where I was going. The result was that I nearly bumped into someone.

'On a collision course again, Kate?' It was Nick's voice. 'You seem to be making a habit of it.'

There was no one I could have wanted to see more, and it seemed like a miracle.

CHAPTER FIVE

NICK was already striding on his way when I put out a hand to detain him.

'Can you stop a minute, *please*? I'm in such awful trouble——'

'You what?' He frowned and said, quite irritably for him, 'What on earth are you on about, Kate?'

'Last night. I was late back and——'

'Late back from where?'

'From Glendale, of course,' I said blankly. 'Had you forgotten where I went yesterday?'

'Actually I had for the moment.' His frown grew blacker. 'I told that young idiot to get you back in good time, or was it your fault for staying too long with your family?'

Before I could deny indignantly that I'd been to blame, a little group of nurses came round the corner and divided to pass us.

'We can't talk here,' Nick continued. 'Are you just going for coffee? I'll join you in the canteen in a few minutes.'

We separated and I hurried on, not as much cheered by the encounter as I might have been, because I'd felt Nick didn't really want to be bothered with my affairs just then.

He turned up as he'd promised, though, and joined me at a small table where I sat alone. I noticed one or two curious glances directed towards us. After all, it wasn't every day that consultants drank coffee with very junior nurses.

'Now,' he said a little impatiently, 'tell me all about it, Kate.'

So I explained exactly what had happened, but I glossed over Jeremy's sleepiness and concentrated on the failure of the plugs.

'It wasn't *really* anybody's fault,' I finished. 'Do you think there's any hope the Senior Nursing Officer will appreciate that?'

'How should I know how her mind will work?' Nick glanced over my shoulder. 'Jeremy's just come in. I'll get him to come here and give an account of himself.'

71

A moment later he came over with his coffee and pulled up a vacant chair from another table. Nick tackled him at once.

'What's all this, Jeremy? I thought you were the sort of bloke who could be relied on, but Kate's landed in a right mess because you didn't start back from Glendale in plenty of time.'

Jeremy gave me a quick glance and I thought I saw reproach in his eyes. From the way the attack had been worded he must think I'd blamed it all on him.

'What have you got to say for yourself?' Nick demanded.

'Only that we did start back in good time—sir. The car was running well and I wasn't to know the plugs would let us down.'

'It's always likely to happen with an old banger like yours, but it wouldn't have mattered if you'd allowed a sensible margin for that sort of thing.'

Jeremy stirred his coffee vigorously and remained silent. I was beginning to wish I hadn't told Nick anything about it. It couldn't be much fun for his houseman to be scolded like a schoolboy hauled up in front of the headmaster—and with me there too.

'Don't say any more, Nick,' I begged. 'It can't do any good now, and I honestly don't think it was Jeremy's fault.'

'Thank you for those few kind words.' Jeremy

drained his cup quickly and stood up. 'I'll get back to work if you'll excuse me, sir.'

Nick made a gesture of dismissal and drank some of his own coffee, grimacing as he did so.

'This stuff gets more awful every day, but I suppose when I was Jeremy's age I'd have been thankful enough for it. We never had time to take a mid-morning break in those days—worked far too hard even to think of it.'

I burst out laughing. 'You're talking as though you were ninety! It's not so long since you were a houseman.'

His lips twitched into a reluctant smile. 'Only six years. I've been very lucky.'

'You've been very clever! Simon was most impressed when I told him of your success. I think he might even have been a bit jealous.'

'He deliberately chose the life of a country G.P.'

'Oh yes—I don't think he regrets it. But he was terribly sorry you weren't able to drive me to Glendale—everybody was disappointed not to see you.'

I waited hopefully. Would he give me just a hint of what it was which had kept him in London?

But all Nick said was, 'I'll make an effort to go north some time next year, after my divorce has come through.'

It occurred to me, for the first time, that it might be the break-up of his marriage which made him reluctant to visit old friends. He wasn't the sort to tolerate failure and he would want his personal life to be as successful as his professional one before he was satisfied.

I was flung back into the present with a bump as I suddenly noticed the time. I was in enough trouble without being late back to the ward.

'I'll have to go now.' I sprang to my feet. 'Thanks, Nick—I'll be seeing you.'

'Let me know how it goes,' he called after me. 'And if you have any difficulty in getting yourself believed I'll put in a word.'

I didn't know what influence he was likely to have with Miss Ferguson, but I felt comforted by his promise.

I just made it to the ward in time. Jeremy was there, talking to a new admission who had come in for observation, and I was sent to join him so that I could make out the chart.

Kevin was seventeen and he had a long history of abdominal pains which had so far not been diagnosed. His G.P. had referred him to the hospital in despair.

The boy certainly looked ill, with a pale face, shadows under his eyes and long lank hair of a mousey brown. He complained constantly as Jeremy palpated his stomach, winced dramatically and generally made a fuss.

'Do you *have* to prod like that?' he grumbled. 'I'm fed up with being messed about, and so you'd

74

be if you were as sore as I am.'

'I expect I would,' Jeremy agreed calmly, 'but I hope I'd understand it was necessary. If we don't find out exactly where the pain is, how can we set about getting it better?'

'It's all over me, I tell you.' Kevin winced again. 'What will they do to me, Doctor? Have I got to have an operation?'

'We don't know yet. It depends on what's wrong with you.'

I asked him the name of his next-of-kin so I could fill it in on the record we kept in the office.

'Nobody!' Seeing my blank look, he raised his voice so that patients in nearby beds turned to stare. 'I haven't got any kin. Is that plain enough for you or do I have to spell it out?'

'There's no need to speak to the nurse like that,' Jeremy told him curtly. 'Everybody is asked that question when they come into hospital. Do you really mean you're completely alone in the world?'

'That's what I said.'

'But you must have been living somewhere, and perhaps your landlady wouldn't mind if you gave her name. It doesn't have to be a relation, in spite of the wording of the question.'

Kevin burst into a cackle of amusement but stopped abruptly as the pain caught him. 'Don't make me laugh! That old cow wouldn't care if I was fished out of the Thames, so long as I'd paid my rent.'

He glanced at me and then looked up at Jeremy, and I got the impression he was actually boasting.

'I tried it once,' he went on, 'but I kept thinking about how cold the water would be and wondering how long it would take to drown. And then while I was hesitating a policeman came along and took me away.'

'You must have been terribly unhappy,' I burst out impulsively, 'to want to do a thing like that.'

Kevin looked me up and down and raised his eyebrows. 'What d'you know about it? I don't reckon you know what unhappiness is.'

'That's enough!' Jeremy said sharply. He slipped his pen into the pocket of his white coat and straightened up. 'Have you got all the information you need, Nurse—with one exception?'

'Yes, thank you.' I hung the chart on the end of the bed and moved away. Halfway down the central corridor between the rooms I found Jeremy was just behind me.

'You weren't very sympathetic with that poor boy,' I told him reproachfully. 'Being alone in the world yourself, I should have thought you'd have understood how he felt.'

'I don't know what makes you imagine I wasn't sympathetic, Kate. For your information, I understand exactly how Kevin feels, but it's not a houseman's job to go around having prolonged heart-to-heart talks with the patients. For one thing, there just isn't time.'

'No, but——' I began doubtfully, and Jeremy interrupted me quickly.

'He'll get psychiatric treatment before he leaves Northleigh, that's for sure, but at present we're only concerned with trying to find out if his pains have a psychosomatic cause.'

'Meaning?'

'That there's no physical reason for them, like ulcers or hiatus hernia or any of the other abdominal troubles.' He changed the subject abruptly. 'Have you seen Miss Ferguson yet?'

I shook my head. 'I've got to wait until tomorrow. She's busy.'

At that moment Sister came out of one of the rooms and said sharply, 'Have you nothing to do except gossip with Dr Bradford, Nurse Wilding?'

I muttered, 'Yes, Sister—sorry, Sister,' and scuttled away.

Somehow I got through the rest of that day without getting into any sort of trouble. My interview was fixed for eleven o'clock in the morning and I spent an agitated few minutes in the locker room making sure my appearance was all it should be. Clean dress, fresh cap exactly balanced, the minimum of make-up, ladderless tights and well-polished shoes—I had done all I could to create a good impression. Nevertheless, my eyes stared back at me from the mirror, seeming larger than usual, and there was the sour taste of fear in my mouth.

On the way to the Senior Nursing Officer's rooms near the front entrance of the hospital I worked hard at bolstering up my courage. A woman of so much experience must surely be familiar with the unreliability of housemen's cars. She would understand it hadn't been my fault.

By the time I got there I'd reasoned myself into a state bordering on optimism, but a fifteen-minute wait in the outer office reduced my spirits to zero again. When I at last entered the large elegant room, with pictures on the walls and a bowl of bronze chrysanthemums on the desk, I was very much aware of an uncomfortable thudding in the region of my heart.

Miss Ferguson was in her forties, with a pale skin and dark hair just streaked with grey. She wore a navy blue dress, very beautifully cut, and no cap. Her eyes were the most penetrating I had ever encountered and I remembered them from my previous meeting with her—the day my mother and I came up for the preliminary interview, before I was admitted to the training school.

'Well, Nurse Wilding?' She studied me with a cool unsmiling gaze. 'You have broken one of the most important rules at Northleigh, but no doubt you have some explanation to offer?'

I'd been rehearsing what I would say and I rushed into my speech at breathless speed, but I didn't say anything about Jeremy being a substitute for Nick. The less complicated my story, the better I would be able to put it over.

Miss Ferguson heard me without interruption, and then she said coldly, 'You realise, of course, that I am bound to conclude one of two things. Either you foolishly left your home much too late, without allowing for possible incidents such as you've described; or, you wasted time on the return journey because you were enjoying the company of your boy-friend. Which was it?'

'It wasn't either, Miss Ferguson,' I burst out indignantly. 'Jeremy's not my boy-friend—not in the way you mean. He's just a—just a friend.'

She raised her eyebrows and looked disbelieving, and I added passionately, 'It's true—honestly it is. We wouldn't have stopped at all if he hadn't been so sleepy he was afraid of dropping off at the wheel.'

That seemed to impress her, I was glad to note. It was well known to be dangerous to drive when you felt sleepy.

'Had the car been giving no signs of trouble until then?' she enquired.

'It'd been going marvellously all day. And we did leave Glendale in good time—or, at least, we thought we had.' I gazed at her beseechingly.

'I think you're telling the truth, Nurse,' she said after a long stare which I did my best to meet without flinching. 'But you must admit it's most unfortunate to have this sort of thing happen so early in your nursing career. I shall have to punish you—you realise that? Young nurses *must* understand that our rules are based on good sense and are there to be obeyed without question.'

'I was expecting to be punished,' I told her cheerfully. 'But I was terribly scared you might sack me.'

She smiled for the first time. 'You would regard that as unnecessarily severe, Nurse?'

'Well—yes, I certainly would.' I turned pink with embarrassment. 'I'm sorry, I shouldn't have said that. I only meant I couldn't bear to leave the hospital; besides, my parents would be absolutely furious with me.'

'Your family has close connections with Northleigh, I believe,' Miss Ferguson said thoughtfully.

So she'd been doing her homework. Perhaps that was why I'd been handled gently on the whole.

My punishment wasn't all that bad. I must be in by ten o'clock for the next two weeks. No late passes for any reason whatsoever.

Incoherent with thanks, I got myself out of the room and hurried back to the ward, just managing not to run.

I hadn't told anybody about the trouble I was in except Prunella and Sister Battle, and yet everybody seemed to know I'd been interviewed by Miss Ferguson. They were obviously curious, but one glance at my face must have told them my world had been straightened out.

Only Jean Sadler actually asked what crime I'd committed and I said briefly that I'd overrun my late pass.

'You got off lightly,' she told me. 'Not so very long ago a nurse in the set senior to mine was late and they sacked her. Of course, she wasn't much good as a nurse. I can't think why she got accepted in the first place.'

Did 'they' think I had the makings of a good nurse? Or was it only my family history which had saved me? I found myself hoping very hard it might have been my nursing ability.

Perhaps it served me right to be taken down a peg. About half-an-hour later I was sent to take out some stitches from a patient who'd had a gall bladder operation. By this time I was quite experienced at this particular job and I approached the man with confidence, my scissors at the ready.

Unfortunately he had very loose flabby flesh and, though I was as careful as I knew how, I somehow managed to get the scissors caught in a fold of skin when I was removing the last stitch.

The patient let out a yell which must have been

heard all over the ward, and Staff Nurse Denman came to see what was the matter.

'She cut me!' the man groaned. 'Cut me with her scissors—you can see the blood.'

And, to my horror, there really was a tiny scarlet streak on the yellowish skin. I withdrew, greatly mortified, and Staff glanced at me reproachfully before soothing the patient's injured feelings and applying a small piece of plaster to the physical injury.

I could have done without Jeremy's presence in the ward at that particular moment.

'What was all that in aid of?' he asked when I met him near the desk.

'Just a trifling incident,' I said airily. 'Did you want something?'

'Only to take another look at Kevin.' He began to move towards the end room and lowered his voice. 'And also to ask how you got on when the Senior Nursing Officer interviewed you.'

'Okay.' I was by now absolutely fed up with people asking me questions about my return from Glendale. As far as I was concerned the matter was closed. 'I can't have a late pass for two weeks, that's all.' I suddenly burst into a giggle. 'It was quite funny in a way. She took it for granted you were my boy-friend.'

Jeremy didn't say anything for a moment and then he flung back at me, his face utterly deadpan,

'I suppose you soon told her she'd got it all wrong?'

'Of course I did.'

As I glanced at his stony expression, I remembered that passionate interlude in the car. More than ever I felt sure that he'd been dreaming and was imagining I was somebody else.

'Have they found out the cause of Kevin's pains?' I asked.

'Not yet. They don't seem to have any physical cause and the boss is fairly certain they're a cry for help from the mind rather than the body.'

I could see what he meant and I looked sympathetically at the boy when we reached his bed, determined not to let him ruffle me.

Kevin looked up with a scowl. If Jeremy sometimes seemed to have a chip on his shoulder, then this patient was carrying a whole load of firewood. He had a grudge against everything and everybody, and just now particularly against the hospital.

'I've been here twenty-four hours,' he grumbled, 'and nobody's done a bloody thing except poke my stomach until I'm so sore I could scream.'

'It sometimes takes much longer than twenty-four hours to find out what's wrong with a patient,' Jeremy said calmly. He picked up the chart and studied it. 'What happened to your parents?' he asked without looking at Kevin.

'My Mum went off with another bloke, didn't she, and she took the two younger ones with her, and then my Dad took up with a girl the same age as my sister.'

'And then?'

'Glynnis—that's my sister—got married and I left home and went to live on my own, but I was always having these pains and feeling sick and I had to give up work.'

'Couldn't you go and live with your sister?'

'She doesn't want me, and there's no room anyway. They've only got a bed-sitter.'

I butted in before I could stop myself. 'If you've got all these relations, you shouldn't have told me you had no next-of-kin.'

Two spots of angry colour appeared in Kevin's white cheeks. 'I don't want anybody told about me. I've got a right to choose, haven't I?'

'Of course you have.' Jeremy moved away from the bed and gestured to me to follow him. 'Why on earth did you have to say that, Kate, just as I'd got him talking?' he demanded in an undertone.

'Sorry—I didn't think!' I rallied quickly. 'It was only yesterday you said you never had time to talk to patients.'

'So I did. Well, it so happens that I had a few minutes to spare this morning.'

I let him have the last word and went off to do some work.

When I went off duty at five o'clock I remembered that there were still two people who would expect to be told the results of my interview with Miss Ferguson—Prunella and Nick. Luckily my friend was off at five o'clock too and so there was no problem about putting her in the picture.

'It's a good thing you didn't have to ask Nick for help,' she said when she'd congratulated me on my escape. 'She might have thought it a bit odd.'

'Why on earth should she? We're friends!' I stared at her indignantly.

'Be your age, love. She couldn't possibly approve of a friendship between a young nurse and a consultant about twelve years older. It's not as though his wife was around—in fact, I heard on the grapevine today that there's to be a divorce. Is it true?'

'Y-yes, he did mention it,' I said reluctantly.

'There you are then! You'll have to be doubly careful,' Prunella told me triumphantly.

I thought she was talking a load of rubbish, but I didn't say so. As I changed the subject it suddenly occurred to me that twice that day I'd protested that somebody—a male each time—was only a friend. Neither time was it exactly true.

CHAPTER SIX

'WHAT shall we do this evening?' Prunella asked, and went on to answer her own question. 'There's a good film on the telly. Let's go downstairs and watch it.'

I was willing to settle for the film, but somehow I couldn't concentrate on it. I kept thinking about Jeremy and Nick and wondering how I really felt about both of them. My relationship with Jeremy was far too tempestuous to be called friendship and at times I really disliked him. Certainly one thing was for sure—there was nobody better at getting under my skin than he was!

And Nick?

As the pictures unrolled before my eyes and the dialogue clamoured for my wandering attention, I knew that I didn't want to analyse my feeling for Nick.

I kept on thinking about him, though, because he hadn't yet been told the result of my interview with the Senior Nursing Officer. When the film ended I slipped out of the lounge and went along to the phones in the corridor behind the stairs. There were three of them, all with those hoods which are supposed to keep conversations private and usually fail utterly.

I was in luck; nobody else was there and I chose the most distant phone and dialled Nick's number.

He might not be at home, of course; he might be out on some social occasion, or still at Northleigh. And as the phone continued to ring monotonously in my ear I almost concluded that the flat was empty.

I was just going to hang up when I heard the receiver being lifted at the other end. I drew in a quick breath of relief and waited for Nick's deep heart-warming voice—slow, lazy and caressing. Instead I heard a female voice.

'Hullo?'

I was so long gathering my wits that she repeated it, a little impatiently, and I pulled myself together.

'Is—is Mr Marston there, please?'

'He will be in a minute. He's just gone out to the wine shop round the corner. Do you want him to ring you back?'

The voice was rather high and very clear, unfamiliar and quite definitely young. As I hesitated, it spoke again.

'I think he's just coming in. Hang on a minute.'

The receiver was put down and I heard the faint sound of voices. A moment later Nick came on the line.

'Who is it?'

'It's—it's Kate.'

'Oh, I see.' There was an infinitesimal pause and then he said impatiently, 'Well, what can I do for you?'

'I thought'—I broke off to control a slight quiver—'I thought you might be wanting to know how I got on with Miss Ferguson today.'

'Miss Ferguson? Oh yes, of course. I'm sorry, Kate—I'm afraid my wits are wandering. How did it go, then? You don't seem to be locked up on bread and water.'

I gave him the details as briefly as I could, and when I'd finished I felt he really was pleased I'd been let off so lightly. But he obviously didn't want to prolong the conversation and I hung up quickly, so he could get back to his guest.

But was she a guest? Until then I'd taken it for granted, but now I sudddenly wondered if the unknown girl could possibly be Elaine—Nick's wife. Maybe they were considering coming together again? People who'd been planning to divorce sometimes did cool down after a period of separation.

The suggestion was thoroughly disturbing. It was bad enough to know that Nick was entertaining a girl-friend—even though he had every right to do so—but to think she might be his wife was even more distressing.

I was jealous—it was as simple as that.

My emotions were in such a muddle that I went early to bed to try and sort myself out. I wasn't successful, but I did eventually get to sleep.

I was on early duty in the morning, but the frantic bustle which went on then no longer had any terrors for me. I could make a bed as quickly as anyone else now, and I knew which patients needed help with their washing without being told.

Sister came on duty, as gimlet-eyed as ever, and Nick and one or two other surgeons did their usual rounds. Suddenly it was lunchtime, and then the afternoon began and Sister went off duty.

Until then everything had been entirely normal—as far as it ever can be in a hospital ward—but the afternoon was going to be very, very different.

It started in the usual way: Jean and I going round to make sure everyone was settled down comfortably for a nap or a quiet rest. An hour or so later the visitors arrived, streaming in with their parcels of clean laundry, fruit and other offerings. Nearly every bed had at least one person beside it, and in the room at the end of the central corridor only Kevin remained alone.

I always felt sorry for patients who didn't have visitors when the others were talking cheerfully with family or friends, and so I went along to see if he was all right.

'What d'you want?' He scowled at me ferociously, but I thought I saw the glint of tears and I tried not to get annoyed.

'I thought you might like someone to talk to for a few minutes.' I busied myself straightening the bedcovers, more as an excuse for remaining than because they needed it. Anyone as lifeless as Kevin was unlikely to get his bed in a muddle.

He shouldn't really have been in bed, since he wasn't exactly ill, but he had refused to get up and Sister hadn't thought it worth a tussle of wills to insist.

'What the hell gave you that daft idea?' he demanded. 'Do me a favour—go away and leave me alone. I don't want any Florence Nightingales around here.'

'I'm too new to think of myself like that.' I was determined not to get ruffled. 'If you don't want to talk, would you like me to find you something to read? The library isn't due till tomorrow, but there are plenty of paperbacks on the shelves in the day room.'

I paused for a reply, but Kevin merely assumed a martyred expression and remained silent, and I added rather less patiently, 'I should have thought anything would be better than just lying there staring into space and thinking about your sore tummy.'

To my surprise he suddenly shed his air of languor.

'I reckon you've got a point there, Nurse—and I

don't mean what you do.' His eyes, pale blue and hostile, stared into mine. 'And now leave me alone, for God's sake. I've had just about as much as I can stand.'

Far from cheering him up, my presence seemed merely to be aggravating his black mood. I gave a final pat to the bedspread, produced a smile with some effort, and went to help serve tea.

Most of the visitors stayed until the last possible minute, and a few always tried to snatch a little extra time, so that we had to remind them politely that they must go.

'I think there's still somebody lingering in the end room,' Staff Nurse Denman told me. 'Go along and chivvy her off, Nurse, please.'

This was the room where Kevin had the bed near the window on one side. I had just reached the open door when I met a little woman with a white face and staring eyes. I opened my mouth to tell her she'd overstayed her time, but her expression halted the words on my lips.

'What's the matter, Mrs—er——?' I asked quickly.

A swift glance showed me that her husband was sitting up in bed looking as fit as could be expected after a major operation, but he also had a look of horror on his face. The bed next to him was empty and also the one opposite, because the patients were in the day room.

I did a double take. There were *three* empty beds. Kevin had obviously gone off to the toilet. Then why did the couple look so upset?

All these thoughts flashed through my mind during the fractional pause which the woman required to master her agitation sufficiently to tell me what was wrong.

'That boy, Nurse—he's gone! One minute he was in bed and the next he was out of it and making for the window——'

'The window!' My eyes left her face and switched to the big expanse of glass at the other end of the room. Two sections of it could be opened by tilting. Theoretically it was impossible for anyone to squeeze through but . . .

'I dunno how he did it,' the visitor went babbling on, 'but he made it seem so easy. Of course being young makes a difference—thin too——'

'Are you trying to tell me Kevin climbed out?' I flung myself across the room and tossed the questions at her over my shoulder. 'Why on earth didn't you *do* something?'

'How could *I* stop him, Nurse? He's a tall lad when he stands up—taller than you'd think—and I'm on the small side myself—and my husband, he couldn't do anything——'

I had reached the window and was staring out. A tall thin figure in striped pyjamas was already halfway along a narrow brick parapet, with a drop of two floors on one side and a sloping roof on the other. Ahead of him there was a higher building which housed the theatres, and an ancient iron ladder led straight up the side. I didn't know what its purpose was; maybe it was a rough and ready fire escape from the hospital's Victorian past, and perhaps someone in danger of death by burning might find the courage to use it.

Or someone crazy enough to be *seeking* death.

I climbed on the chair Kevin had left handy and called through the open space.

'Kevin! Come back—please, please come back!'

It was a waste of breath and I knew it. Frantically I yelled at the little woman hovering behind me, 'Don't just stand there—fetch help! Tell Staff what's happened—maybe she'll know what to do.'

Then, not stopping to think but acting entirely instinctively, I heaved myself up and scrambled through the narrow aperture.

The cat-walk was a little to the right, but I lowered myself to the sill and my feet found it without difficulty. I stood up, took a deep breath and set out in pursuit.

I've never been afraid of heights and now the tough training given me by my brothers stood me in good stead. All my life I had been accustomed to climb trees, scramble among the rocky tops of the highest parts of the moors, and walk upright and fearlessly along narrow ridges. A solid brick

93

parapet eighteen inches wide was nothing to me and I moved confidently and at a good pace.

But Kevin had had a good start and he was already climbing the ladder. It seemed as if the grim purpose which was urging him to seek a higher point was giving him superhuman strength and courage.

I didn't like the look of that ladder at all, and I hesitated at the bottom. Should I make another attempt to speak to him, or would that put him in greater danger by breaking the trance he seemed to be in? A moment's thought convinced me that the only possible course was to go after him.

I put both hands on the iron sides of the ladder and started the ascent.

Even now I wasn't scared of being so high up; my only concern was the ladder itself, whether it might break away from the wall or the rusty iron might snap. It was obviously best not to think about it, and I tried to empty my mind of all thoughts except the need to move hands and feet in a slow regular rhythm. Not until I was near the top did I even glance up, and then I discovered Kevin had made it and vanished onto the roof.

My arms ached and my hands were sore from the rough metal. I had a sudden desperate need to get to the end myself and I increased speed slightly. A moment later I too was struggling onto the roof.

Gasping and trembling a little, I looked round for Kevin, terrified that he might already have thrown himself down. But he was still there, and I saw that he'd climbed onto the edge of a skylight and was sitting there, white-faced and panting, staring about him.

I didn't know what to do, whether to approach nearer or try to get and hold his attention from my present position, and as I hesitated I glanced back the way I had come.

All the windows of Fleming Ward which overlooked the scene were lined with faces. Moving along the cat-walk at a steady speed was Jeremy.

An enormous wave of relief washed over me. Jeremy would join me up on the roof and talk Kevin into giving up his plan; the responsibility of saving a crazy boy from suicide would no longer be mine alone.

I watched until he reached the ladder and then I couldn't bear to look any longer. Besides, I had Kevin to think of. At all costs I must keep his mind off his purpose and that meant talking to him.

I didn't know any of the right things to say and so I started in an ordinary conversational way.

'There's a marvellous view up here, isn't there?'

It sounded utterly idiotic, but a boy hell-bent on death was right outside my experience. I just had to play it by ear.

Kevin didn't seem particularly surprised to see me. 'I didn't come up here to look at the view,' he informed me scornfully.

'It's worth looking at, all the same.' I pointed away to the left. 'There's Tower Bridge. Doesn't it look super from here?'

His blank gaze shifted slightly in the direction of my extended arm. I took the opportunity to move a little nearer, so that there should be room for Jeremy.

Against a background noise of distant traffic and the small sounds made by the wind—which fortunately was little more than a breeze—I could hear heavy breathing and the slow scrape of feet on metal. Jeremy must be quite close now. I nerved myself for the ordeal of watching him struggling onto the roof, and at the same time longed to be able to transfer responsibility to him.

As I racked my brains to think of something else to say to Kevin, a seagull arrived from the direction of the river and alighted quite close. It stared at us with its bright uncaring eyes and then flew away again.

'It must wonder what on earth we're doing here,' I suggested and then caught my breath in alarm. Of all the daft things to say when I was trying to keep his mind off his intentions!

But Kevin made no move. He merely eyed me cynically and said, 'I dunno what *you*'re doing up

here and you haven't half got yourself in a mess.'
His eyes flickered past me. 'Gawd—here's another!
It's getting like Piccadilly Circus on this roof-top.'

Jeremy had made it at last. His face was rust-streaked and glistening with sweat, and there was a sort of desperation in the way his hands scrabbled for a hold. It occurred to me that a boy brought up in the East End of London might not feel as much at home in high places as I did.

'Take it easy,' I told him anxiously. 'This bit is rather dicey.'

He managed it somehow and sprawled on the roof at my side, looking so pale that I felt quite concerned.

'It's quite safe here,' I said encouragingly, 'and not all that uncomfortable, as a matter of fact.'

Jeremy smiled in a twisted sort of way. 'You've got a rum idea of comfort, Kate.' He lowered his voice and spoke close to my ear. 'They've sent for the Fire Service and in the meantime we've got to keep him talking.'

'That's what I've been trying to do.' I glanced across at the pyjama-clad figure sitting on the edge of the skylight and I noticed a shiver. If Kevin didn't get pneumonia after this escapade it'd be a miracle.

Assuming he didn't end up lying broken and bleeding on the concrete below.

To our alarm he was beginning to fidget a bit

and he said irritably, 'If you've quite finished whispering together, I wish you'd go away and leave me in peace.'

'I can't go just yet, mate,' Jeremy told him, 'because I came up specially to tell you something.'

'I don't want to hear anything you've got to say. I had enough of that in the ward—so scram!'

'But this is different from anything I've already told you——' Jeremy broke off and I felt his body grow tense as he listened.

Very faintly on the wind there came the sound of a fire siren. It didn't necessarily mean that help was on the way—sirens occurred dozens of times every day in London—but I couldn't help feeling hopeful.

'Can you see anything?' Jeremy muttered.

'No. Can you?' I answered in the same tone.

'I—can't look down. To put it bluntly, I daren't.'

I already knew he didn't share my lucky ability to perch on roof-tops and ignore the little matter of gravity. He'd been frightened, very likely, the whole time he was climbing up from the ward. But he'd come just the same.

'You're whispering again,' Kevin complained. 'What's this you want to tell me, then?'

There was actually just a tinge of curiosity in his voice and I felt Jeremy had scored a small victory, though whether he'd actually got anything to tell Kevin I didn't know. I looked at him hopefully and saw that he was choosing his words with care.

'You think you're all alone in the world, don't you? Well, that makes two of us—except that I really am alone, whereas you've got hordes of relations hidden away, whose existence you don't want to acknowledge. I reckon I know much more about loneliness than you do.'

The siren was much louder now but still Kevin didn't seem to have noticed it. He was staring at Jeremy in astonishment.

'Garn! You're a doctor—you don't have my sort of background.'

'How do you know I don't?' Jeremy demanded.

I was sure now that the fire engine had stopped at Northleigh. I could hear voices and the sound of machinery, and suddenly the top of a fire escape appeared with a man on it. I held my breath in alarm; if Kevin saw it too soon he might remember what he'd come up to the roof for—and throw himself off.

I saw him shiver again as he debated how to answer Jeremy's question and I burst out impulsively,

'Why on earth didn't you put your dressing gown on before you came up here? You're absolutely freezing!'

'Didn't think of it,' he said absently. 'I got a sudden impulse and took off in case anybody tried to stop me.'

Before either of us could continue the conversation another voice spoke suddenly from a few feet away.

'Well, well, well—quite a party up here! I reckon you've been sitting in the cold long enough, all the lot of you. Who's coming down first?'

'Better take Kevin.' Jeremy pointed to the white-faced boy. 'He's probably got pneumonia as it is.'

I held my breath and Jeremy's knuckles tensed. Kevin was hesitating and the fireman directed at him a string of encouraging remarks. It was obvious he'd been in this sort of situation before.

Slowly and carefully the boy stood up. He accepted a helping hand and was taken onto the fire escape, held firmly in a strong grip.

'I'll be back for you two in a minute,' the fireman called.

We watched them sink out of sight and then looked at each other.

'He actually went down without any fuss at all!' I gasped. 'It almost seemed like he was glad. Do you think he ever meant to commit suicide?'

'I think he did when he started out, but after he got up here he changed his mind. Very likely you had something to do with it. He could see that somebody cared enough to come after him.' Jeremy's hand clutched mine and tightened its grip. 'It was crazy, Kate—you might have been killed.'

I was both pleased and embarrassed at his words. 'It was nothing—honestly! The only dangerous bit was the ladder and that was more secure than it looked.' I tried to explain how easy I found that sort of thing.

'You're very lucky,' Jeremy said in a low, strained voice. 'I don't mind telling you I was sick with nerves, both for you and myself.' He smiled faintly. 'I didn't know at first you were as agile as a cat.'

We sat there holding hands until the fireman came back. I wanted very badly to say Jeremy could go down first, but I knew it would hurt his pride and so I kept quiet. The descent on the fire escape was a new experience and I would have enjoyed it if I hadn't been so worried about Jeremy up there on the roof.

I didn't feel really safe until he was down on the ground beside me.

CHAPTER SEVEN

QUITE a large crowd of people had gathered to watch our rescue from the roof. As Jeremy joined me a spontaneous burst of clapping arose, and his pale dirt-streaked face turned bright red with embarrassment.

I was feeling much the same myself and, to hide it, I asked him if he knew how filthy his face was.

'Your own's the same, Kate, and as for your apron——' He grinned down at me. 'Isn't there a rule about never leaving the ward without removing it first?'

I laughed shakily and wished my legs would stop trembling. It was reaction, I suppose, but I was more wobbly now than I'd been at any time during the adventure.

'What have they done with Kevin?' I asked as we walked towards the side door of the hospital.

'I expect he's back, inside, but in a different ward. If he isn't ill as a result of this afternoon he'll probably be transferred to the psychiatry unit almost at once.'

'And we shall never know what happens to him eventually,' I said regretfully. 'That's the worst of being a nurse. You get to know people so intimately and then they go right out of your life.'

'It would be impossible to keep up with everybody,' Jeremy reminded me. 'And you'd wear yourself out doing it.'

We had reached the door. Inside was a short corridor which at that time of day was completely empty. I was beginning to wonder if it wouldn't have been more sensible to go straight to the

Nurses' Home to change, and it wasn't until I felt Jeremy's grip on my arm that I realised he'd stopped.

'Kate——' He broke off and swallowed, and when he continued speaking his voice was shaking. 'I never want to live through an afternoon like this again in my whole life. Once is quite enough!'

'I don't exactly want to repeat it,' I said thoughtfully. Looking up at him, I went on, 'I was so relieved when you joined me on the roof, but I'm sorry you had that horrible climb.'

'Somebody had to go after you. Staff was doing her nut when she realised what had happened. She might even have gone after you herself.'

He was still holding on to me, and suddenly he picked up a handful of my apron, selected a bit that wasn't too dirty and wiped my face with it. As I gazed at him in amazement he rubbed his own vigorously and then let it go.

'That's better! I like to be able to see a girl when I kiss her—and I'm going to kiss you *hard*. It's the only possible ending to an adventure like we've just had.'

And as he held me tightly and pressed his mouth down on mine, I knew that I felt in total agreement with him. It *was* the only possible celebration of our safe return to ground level.

When he let me go I was breathless and flushed, and my cap—which had remained miraculously in place until then—had slipped down onto the back of my neck. I hurriedly got it back into position and Jeremy ran his hands through his hair and smoothed it down. He didn't look too bad now, but I was still in a complete mess.

'Thank goodness Sister isn't in this afternoon!' I set off at a rapid pace.

'I bet she'll have something to say to you when she comes on again,' came his voice from behind me.

'Thanks very much—that's most encouraging!' I flung at him over my shoulder.

Our relationship seemed to have returned to normal, but I didn't know whether to be glad or sorry. Not that I had much time to think about it, for I was soon in the midst of a considerable fuss.

Staff Nurse Denman was the first to comment on my behaviour, but she couldn't make up her mind whether to scold me or congratulate me on my 'amazing courage'. I told her I hadn't been brave at all, but she brushed it aside.

The nurses all wanted to know what had happened up on the roof and refused to believe me when I said, 'Nothing much. We talked about the view.'

Then Sister Battle had her turn, and she gave me a lecture on being impulsive.

'If you'd stopped to think, Nurse Wilding, I'm sure you would never have set off on such a crazy escapade.'

I tried to explain about my brothers and the way I'd been brought up, but she brushed it aside impatiently.

'That has very little to do with it. You must know that you took a terrible risk. Your obvious duty was to call for help and not to set off in pursuit yourself. In all my long experience of nursing I have never, *never* known a young student nurse to behave so crazily.'

She glared at me and then, to my utter astonishment, produced a grim smile. 'Your friends will probably tell you that you showed great courage and I am bound to concur with that opinion. You may go, Nurse.'

I walked out treading on air, but it wasn't long before I came down to earth with a bump as once more I was summoned to the Senior Nursing Officer's presence. I felt nearly as scared as last time and her opening remark didn't make me feel any better.

'I don't think I have ever had to send for a girl *twice* in the first weeks of her training, Nurse Wilding! If you continue to thrust yourself on my notice like this I really don't know what we are going to do with you.'

I stood rigidly with my hands behind my back and looked down at the carpet, and Miss Ferguson went on speaking.

'This time you seem to have been covering yourself with glory, but I should be failing in my duty if I didn't point out to you the foolhardiness of your adventure. You might have been killed.'

I said nervously, 'I'm sorry, Miss Ferguson. I didn't stop to worry about whether it was the right thing to do. At the time it seemed to be the *only* thing.' And again I launched into an account of my childhood.

She listened with more interest than Sister had shown and actually seemed impressed.

'I suppose from your point of view that does make a difference, but I wonder whether you've considered Dr Bradford's side of it? It was undoubtedly the sight of you setting off over the roof-tops which caused him to risk his own life, and I don't think he has had so much experience of heights as you.'

I stared at her in amazement. 'But, Miss Ferguson, it was surely because he wanted to save Kevin that Jeremy—Dr Bradford—came too? I mean, he'd have gone even if I hadn't started first.'

'Perhaps.' But she didn't look as though she believed me. 'I certainly haven't the time just now to enquire into his motives.' Her manner was suddenly much more formal. 'Before you go, Nurse, I must ask for an assurance that you will never attempt anything of the sort again. I sincerely hope the occasion won't arise, but if it does and

106

you happen to be on the spot, you are *not* to take matters into your own hands. Is that clear?'

I said, 'Yes, Miss Ferguson,' adding reflectively, 'I certainly don't want to do it again, because I was so scared I might fail.'

'You certainly didn't fail. In fact, it's very likely that you saved a life. You have a right to feel proud of yourself.'

This time when I was dismissed I was not only treading on air but ten feet tall, but this blissful state only lasted until I got back to the ward, where I found I was in trouble for not being there to help with the evening toilet round.

Jeremy was in one of the rooms, examining an emergency admission, and he raised his eyebrows as I passed near.

'Okay, Kate?'

'Yes, thanks.' I dumped a bowl of water on somebody's locker and was rushing on my way when he spoke again.

'Would you like to go out for a drink later on? Just to celebrate our continued existence?' And, seeing my surprise, he added nonchalantly, 'It doesn't matter if you're busy.'

'I wasn't doing anything special. Thanks, Jeremy, I'd like that.' I flung him a smile and raced back to the sluice.

When I went off duty I soaked for ages in a hot bath and spent some time trying to get my nails looking decent, as they seemed to have collected half the rust off the ladder. As I got ready to meet Jeremy downstairs, I suddenly wondered if Nick had heard about the afternoon's adventure.

Surely he must have? The whole hospital would know by now. I had a sudden longing to talk to him about it and find out whether he went along with the general official opinion of my behaviour, or whether he would tell me how wonderfully brave I'd been. It wasn't true, of course, but I'd have liked to hear him saying it.

If only I'd been going to have a drink with *him* . . .

But no sooner had the thought entered my head than I drew back in shame. It wasn't fair to Jeremy to wish he was somebody else, even though he knew nothing about it.

He was late, which didn't bother me as I understood how difficult housemen found it to keep dates. He arrived in a hurry, looking as though he'd come straight from the ward without even stopping to brush his hair.

'Sorry, Kate—something blew up and I thought I was going to be let in for assisting at an emergency op., but luckily both the registrars were free and Mr Marston said I needn't stay.'

'Was it that new admission?' I asked.

'Yes. He suddenly developed peritonitis. The boss daren't wait until tomorrow.'

We set out together, still talking about the patient whose life Nick was saving at that moment, somewhere in the tall block where we'd sat perched that afternoon. It hardly seemed possible, now, that it had happened, and yet if it hadn't we wouldn't have been going out to celebrate.

At that moment it occurred to me we weren't heading for the usual pub opposite the hospital.

'Where are we going?' I paused on the kerb to let the traffic thunder past and looked enquiringly at Jeremy.

'A little place by the river. It doesn't get full of the hospital mob like the other one. I've already seen Prunella and Mac heading in that direction and they would have teamed up with us.'

'They might have preferred to be on their own,' I suggested, just for the sake of arguing.

'Shouldn't think so. You surely don't imagine they're serious about each other just because they go around together quite a lot?' On the other side of the busy road Jeremy tucked his arm in mine and steered me down a narrow street. 'Hard-working blokes like housemen need a little light relief— such as love—on the side, but nobody in his right mind would let himself get serious. And I should think the same goes for first-year student nurses.'

'Oh yes, of course,' I assured him quickly.

He could hardly have made his point more clear if he'd said outright, 'Don't get ideas, Kate, just because I've kissed you and now I'm taking you out for a drink. It doesn't mean a thing.'

I didn't want it to mean anything. Of course I didn't. But a girl doesn't care for being told so plainly that she's only light relief, and I was most unusually silent all the way to the pub.

When we entered the small saloon bar I looked round approvingly. 'This is much more like a real local than the other place—no plastic flowers or flashing mirrors.'

Jeremy grinned. 'I suppose it reminds you a little of the inn at Glendale? What'll you drink?'

I chose my usual lime-and-lager and he got a beer for himself. As we sat down side-by-side on a high-backed settle my mind reverted to the reason for our being there.

'I wonder how Kevin's feeling now—whether he's glad he was rescued.' I turned my head and looked at Jeremy. 'It was clever of you to tell him you understood how he felt because of your own situation.'

He gave his characteristic shrug. 'It was the only thing I could think of, but I was thankful when the fireman turned up so quickly. I didn't want to go on pouring out my life story. Kevin might have got bored very rapidly.'

'I don't think *I* would get bored,' I ventured. I waited a second and then added, 'Try me and see.'

Jeremy glanced at me in a startled way. He was

so near I could see the tiny golden hairs on his cheeks above where he shaved. I was momentarily side-tracked as I wondered whether his eyes were blue-grey or grey-blue. Just now they looked very blue.

'You know an awful lot about me,' I pointed out, 'but I still only know two things about you. You were born at Northleigh and you haven't a home. You can't get much more basic than that.'

'There's not much to tell.' He was pushing a dead match round and round a large glass ashtray with the tip of his finger, and no longer looking at me. 'My mother was a local girl, but she lit out after my birth and left me to be adopted.' And he added curtly, 'I was illegitimate, of course.'

I couldn't see that mattered very much, but I thought it was sad his mother apparently hadn't tried to keep him.

'So what happened to you? Did you have to go to a home?'

'I was luckier than some,' Jeremy said. 'I got adopted by a couple who had a cheap tailoring business in the city. They made a reasonable living at it, but they had to work very hard. When I was a kid I used to lie awake in bed and hear the sewing machines going far into the night.'

'But where are they now?' I was puzzled. 'Why are you alone in the world?'

'For a very good reason. My adopted mother

111

and father were killed in a coach crash one bank holiday. They were on an outing to Brighton—the only holiday they had all the year.'

'Oh, Jeremy—how awful!' Impulsively I put my hand on his arm. 'But didn't they have any relations?'

'Not that I know of,' he told me. 'Their parents were dead and they'd both been only children. If they had relations once they'd lost touch with them.' He raised his head and his eyes scanned my face briefly. 'I expect you find that hard to understand, with your clannishness and your swarm of brothers, to say nothing of uncles and aunts and cousins.'

'I just can't imagine what it's like to be all alone,' I admitted. 'Nobody caring what happens to you, and not a single person in the world to listen when you want to—to pour things out.'

'You soon get so you *don't* want to pour things out,' Jeremy said.

I couldn't imagine that either and I asked him how old he was when his parents were killed.

'I was twenty, just finishing my second year at the Northleigh Medical School.' He paused and then added quietly. 'It was a shattering blow. I—I was very fond of them.'

We were both silent for a moment and then I asked another question.

'Have you ever thought of trying to trace your

mother? It's possible for adopted children to do that now, I believe?'

'Of course I've thought of it! And I tried it too, but she'd vanished without trace.' He smiled bleakly. 'Maybe it was just as well—we might not have liked each other at all. Let me get you another drink.'

When he came back we didn't refer any more to his life story. Instead I found myself being asked for further details about my own family.

'Are all your brothers married?'

'Robert isn't. He's the youngest and still playing the field. All the others are settled in matrimony and three of them have children.'

Jeremy listened with surprising patience while I gave the names and ages of all my nephews and nieces, and then he said with a tinge of envy, 'It's wonderful for your father to have his eldest son join him in the practice.'

'Yes.' I remembered that he'd told me he fancied general practice himself. 'You'll probably end up as a country doctor if that's what you really want.'

'Perhaps, but it's a long way off yet. This is only my second houseman job.' Jeremy spread out his hands and looked at them. 'I'm not neat-fingered enough for surgery. I haven't done much so far, of course, but I've a strong feeling it's not for me.'

'It must be a terrible feeling the first time you pick up a scalpel and cut somebody's flesh.

113

Weren't you scared?'

Jeremy's face twisted into an expressive grimace. 'You bet I was! And it didn't help to have the boss glaring at me over his mask. He has very expressive eyes, as perhaps you've noticed since you know him so well?'

I said that I had, and added that I couldn't imagine Nick being impatient with a nervous houseman.

'You'd be surprised!' Jeremy laughed in a sarcastic sort of way which I didn't much care for.

I was just going to rush to Nick's defence when I was overtaken by a tremendous yawn and immediately my companion's attitude changed.

'Sorry you're so bored!' he said stiffly.

I flung him an exasperated look. 'Don't be like that! I'm *not* bored, but I soon shall be if you're going to get that chip on your shoulder again.'

He turned right round and stared at me. 'Have I got a chip, Kate? I didn't know.'

'Of course you have—an outsize one. That's why you're so sympathetic with Kevin. You're two of a kind, except that *you*'re not suicidal—at least I hope not.'

'So do I,' he said emphatically. 'Suicide is a feeble way out and makes a lot of trouble for other people.' He reverted to my accusation. 'I'm sorry if I've given you the impression I've got a grudge against the world. It's true that I do sometimes feel a bit that way, but I imagined I'd kept it to myself.'

'If you really want to know,' I told him frankly, 'I noticed it that first evening we met.'

'Good God! I shall have to be careful in future, that's for sure.' He smiled and put his hand on mine where it lay on the table. 'Will you give me another chance, Kate?'

I said the first thing which came into my head.

'The way you choose to go around hasn't anything to do with me.'

There was a sudden silence. All around us the noise of the pub went on, people laughing and talking, but Jeremy and I seemed isolated in a little oasis of our own. I knew he was staring at me but I didn't want to meet his eyes because of what I might see in them. I had a horrible feeling that I'd hurt him and I wished I could recall that flat statement.

It had been unnecessarily blunt, and the only merit it possessed lay in its truth.

'I see,' Jeremy said quietly. 'Shall we go? It's been rather a long day, with a very great deal happening.'

I got up without a word and led the way to the door. We walked silently through the narrow streets, back to the wide road where the hospital stood.

'Thank you for the drinks,' I said politely when

we came to the turning which led to the Nurses' Home.

'My pleasure.' Jeremy's tone was as formal as mine had been.

I looked up at him and hesitated. With all my heart I longed for a return to the happier relationship we had managed to establish earlier, but I couldn't see how to do anything about it without giving an entirely false impression of my attitude towards him.

It was Jeremy who saved the situation.

I was turning away when he said urgently, 'Just a minute, Kate.' His hand was on my shoulder, twisting me round to face him. 'I'm not letting you go like this, even though we do seem gifted at bringing out the worst in each other.'

I stared up at him in the light of the street lamps and I felt my pulses quicken slightly.

'I don't understand.'

'Actions speak louder than words, as my adopted mother used to tell me when I was a kid. Well, here's an action for you and if you don't like it, then it's just too bad.'

He bent his head and kissed me firmly on the lips, not once but several times.

'This is becoming a habit!' I wriggled free at last and stood poised for flight.

'And it's not a bad habit either,' Jeremy told me cheerfully.

CHAPTER EIGHT

AFTER the excitement of Kevin's flight to the roof-top, life continued fairly normally in Fleming Ward. I worked hard and kept out of Sister's way as much as possible, but as far as the other nurses were concerned I discovered that my prestige had risen. I was still the most junior, still given the most mundane jobs to do, but in some subtle way I was very much more one of them than I'd been before.

And then—quite suddenly it seemed—the time came for me to be moved to a different ward.

It wasn't just me, of course; all our set were getting a move, and one evening when I came off duty Prunella told me the new postings had been put on the board.

'We're both going to medical wards, Kate——'

'That'll make a change,' I interrupted. 'I hope I don't get another Battleaxe for a Sister.'

'I shouldn't think there's another in the whole hospital, but as a matter of fact neither of us will have to worry about ward Sisters for the next two months.'

I looked at her in surprise. 'Why on earth not?'

Prunella made the announcement which she'd

117

obviously been saving up for dramatic effect. 'We're going on night duty—that's why!'

The info brought me up with a jerk. I couldn't bear the thought of having to sleep during the best part of the day, and as for working all through the hours of darkness—the mere suggestion made me wilt.

'It was bound to happen sooner or later,' I said, trying to cheer myself up.

'I wish it hadn't come just now, though. Do you realise we shall still be on nights at Christmas! It'll be hellish!'

But I couldn't be bothered to look that far ahead. I had just remembered something which had lifted my spirits like magic.

'We get four whole days' holiday before our change of ward, don't we? I shall be able to go home!'

I rushed to the phone and rang up my mother to tell her the glad news, and after that I started counting the days. My last day in Fleming Ward came and suddenly I didn't want to leave it, but the feeling vanished the moment I went off duty because tomorrow I was going home.

Or so I thought.

I'd got as far as the bottom of the first flight of stairs in the Nurses' Home when the Warden appeared and told me my mother had rung up and I was to phone her back. I was puzzled but not particularly worried, and I went straight to the phone.

But with Mum's first sentence all my happiness and eager anticipation were totally destroyed.

'I'm so terribly sorry, dear, but I don't think you ought to come tomorrow. Jane and Nicola have gone down with some sort of fever. Both your father and Simon think it may be glandular fever, and I'm sure the hospital wouldn't want you to be in contact with that.'

As I listened I felt quite ill with disappointment. Simon and his wife and children shared my parents' house, which was much too large for two people, and although theoretically they had separate establishments the children were used to running in and out of their grandparents' rooms just as they liked.

'Are you still there, Kate?' Mum asked, and when I managed to produce some sort of strangled sound, she said sympathetically, 'Poor darling—you must be absolutely shattered, but you do agree it would be wrong for you to come, don't you?'

I had to agree. The Senior Nursing Officer would go up the wall if she knew I'd deliberately let myself come into contact with something infectious. Specially if it really was glandular fever.

'Oh, Mum——' my voice broke '—what an utterly ghastly thing to happen! I was so looking forward to my holiday at Glendale.' And, belatedly, I added, 'How are the kids? Do they feel very ill?'

'Not too bad, but they're obviously far from well.' She suddenly became very determinedly cheerful. 'Never mind, Kate—you'll be able to come another time, and we did see you recently when your grandmother died.'

'It'll be after Christmas before I get another four days,' I said gloomily. 'It's just not worth trying to get home when I have my nights off. I'd be falling asleep all the time.'

'How do they arrange night duty now?' she asked.

'Four nights on and two off.'

'We had to do seven nights in a row before we had any time off, but nobody works as hard as they did in the old days, not even nurses.'

We went on talking for a while and then rang off. I replaced the receiver slowly, absurdly wanting to hang on to it as long as possible because it was a link with home. As I turned away towards the entrance hall I had to struggle with tears.

I didn't want to speak to anybody just then; I wanted to be by myself, to come to terms with my disappointment before I was obliged to tell anyone about it.

I pulled my cape round me and went outside, turning blindly down the narrow road which led past the back of the hospital. Various doors and gates led into the hospital complex, but they were all out of bounds for nurses and, as far as I knew, none of us ever used them.

But somebody was coming out of one of the doors—not a nurse but a tall man in a dark suit who was striding along with head bent as though lost in thought.

Suddenly he looked up and saw me.

'Kate! What on earth are you doing wandering about here in the cold?' Nick caught me by the arms and smiled down at me. 'How's the hospital heroine, then? I don't seem to have had a chance to congratulate you on your amazing courage.'

I'd been just the least bit hurt because he hadn't made an opportunity of mentioning my adventure, since everybody else was making such a fuss about it. I hadn't, in fact, had any conversation with him since that unsatisfactory telephone call after I got into trouble for being late.

But none of that mattered now. I was so pleased to meet him that for a moment I couldn't speak. He was the one person I could bear to see just then.

'Is something wrong?' he asked anxiously.

'N-nothing important. It's only that—that——' I gave up trying to control my grief and put both hands over my face, letting the tears trickle through my fingers.

'You wouldn't cry if it really wasn't important.' Nick drew me into the shelter of a doorway. 'Please tell me what's wrong. You haven't been

121

getting into trouble again?'

'No, it's something quite different.' I poured out the whole story. 'I know I'm being childish to mind so much,' I went on, 'but Glendale is such a very special place to me and I'd been so looking forward to going there for a few days.'

'At nineteen it's permissible to behave childishly now and then,' Nick said softly. 'You're lucky you're still young enough to find relief in shedding a few tears.'

There was something strange about his voice as he said that and I peered up into his face, but it was too dark for me to see his expression.

'You sounded as though things had been going wrong with you,' I said diffidently. 'Have you had a disappointment too?'

'Life is full of disappointment, Kate.' His voice had changed again and was slightly mocking. 'We have to learn to take it.'

'For goodness' sake!' I was exasperated with him and didn't hesitate to show it. 'Stop talking like you were an aged uncle giving advice to his niece! You're not all that much older than me and I don't look on you as an uncle.' And inside my own head I added silently, 'Far from it!'

Nick laughed. 'I assure you I don't feel avuncular towards you, Kate. What are you going to do with your holiday now you can't go home?'

I said forlornly, 'I don't know. Stay here and go

out exploring London, I suppose.'

He appeared to be lost in thought and I waited with a slight resurgence of hope. Maybe he'd got a suggestion to make?

I was right about that, but when it came it was so surprising that I was almost struck dumb with amazement.

'It won't be much fun for you to stay at the Nurses' Home and keep all the rules, Kate. Does anybody know about your change of plan?'

'Not yet,' I said. 'It's only just happened.'

'Then don't tell the Warden or any of your friends. Pack your case and set out as though you were going home, but instead come to my flat and stay there.'

It was so unexpected that I quite literally gasped. Nick must have felt my astonishment for he went on hurriedly.

'Don't get me wrong, Kate—my intentions are perfectly honourable!' I saw the flash of his teeth as he smiled in the darkness. 'I have a very small spare room which you'd be welcome to occupy, but you'd have to fill in the days on your own. In the evenings, perhaps, I might be able to take you out once or twice and show you a bit of London nightlife. Would you like that?'

'Oh *yes*!' My tears had dried, even my disappointment was temporarily forgotten. 'I'd *love* it, Nick. You are an angel to have thought of it.'

'I'm no angel, Kate, that's for sure, but you can trust me to behave myself.'

I wasn't *quite* certain I wanted him to behave himself, or not too much anyway, but I kept that private.

'Feeling better now?' he asked.

'I'm fine now, thanks.' I disengaged myself from his clasp. 'Thank you a million times, Nick. And now I think I'd better go in and start packing.'

'Don't forget your winter woollies. It's cold in North Yorkshire at this time of the year!'

We both laughed, and Nick put his hand in his pocket and took out a key.

'Here's my spare key to the flat. Make yourself at home and do just what you like, but be prepared to go out in the evening if I get back in time.'

Impulsively I flung my arms round his neck and kissed him. 'I shall always be grateful to you for this, Nick. See you tomorrow night!'

I sped back to the Nurses' Home ahead of him and went straight upstairs, where I changed out of uniform and began packing.

Just as I'd finished Prunella came in and sat down on my bed.

'Looking forward to your days off?' I asked cheerfully.

She shook her head. 'I might if I'd got somewhere nice to go like you have. You know how much I hate it at home. I suppose you wouldn't like to take me to Glendale with you? It'd be interesting to see that fabulous place after hearing you talking non-stop about it for two months.'

As I looked at her in horror she burst out laughing.

'If you could see your face! I didn't mean it, you idiot. I was just fooling.'

'I'd absolutely love to have you come and stay some time,' I said warmly, rather overdoing the enthusiasm, 'but not at this time of the year. Perhaps next summer——'

'I'll hold you to that.' She got up and stretched. 'I expect you'll be off at crack of dawn to catch your train, but I'm going to have a long lie-in, so don't disturb me. Goodnight, Kate—have fun while you're at home.'

I said I was sure I would and went to bed early myself, to lie awake for hours alternately grieving because I wasn't going to Glendale, and getting myself worked up into a state of excitement because of staying with Nick.

The result was that I slept late and had to creep out of the Nurses' Home long after I would have had to leave to travel north. I picked up a taxi quite quickly and was soon at Nick's flat.

It seemed very strange to let myself in with a key, stranger still to be there on my own. I prowled around for a while, finding out where things were kept so that I could get myself some food without going out if I wanted to. I had the oddest feeling that I was a trespasser and shouldn't be there at all, and eventually I couldn't stand it any longer.

I'd go out and take a bus to the West End, I decided. A spell of window-shopping would be a good way of passing the time until evening.

I enjoyed it, up to a point, but I wished I had somebody with me and I returned to the flat in plenty of time to get ready for the evening, just in case Nick felt like taking me out.

Even if we stayed at home, it would be nice to dress up. And so I put on a dark green velvet skirt and teamed it up with a copper-coloured top which I hoped brought out the lights in my hair.

Nick didn't get back as early as I'd hoped, but at last I heard his key in the lock and I jumped up to greet him. He came striding in, flinging the sitting room door wide, and then halted abruptly.

'Kate! Good God, I'd——' He broke off sharply, but I had a terrible feeling he'd been going to say he'd forgotten I would be there.

The moment passed in a flash and I was soon able to persuade myself I'd imagined it.

'I can't have you all dressed up and nowhere to go.' Nick poured drinks for us both. 'Just give me a few minutes and then I'll be ready. Where would you like to eat?'

126

'I don't know anything about eating out in London.'

'There's a very attractive little *taverna* just off Piccadilly you might enjoy. Do you like Greek food?'

'And where do you suppose I've eaten Greek food in Glendale?' I demanded.

Nick laughed. 'Dear Kate—you never pretend, do you? I find that very refreshing.'

He had a quick shower and then we set out, taking a taxi because he said he didn't like having his intake of alcohol firmly controlled by the breathalyser. As we rode through the brightly-lit streets I couldn't help feeling that the occasion itself was sufficiently intoxicating for me. I didn't need wine to put a crown on my happiness.

I had to drink some, of course, and by the time we left the *taverna* I was in a state which was just the least bit hazy. Nick suggested walking along Piccadilly and I was glad when he slipped his arm through mine as we strolled through the crowds. Nearly everybody we passed seemed to be foreign and wearing something exotic, and strange languages assailed us on every side.

This was Life, I told myself dreamily, and just at that moment I was jolted out of my trance by noticing a girl staring hard at us.

She was slender and very attractive, with pale gold hair, and I felt I'd seen her somewhere before.

As she stood poised on the kerb waiting to cross the road, I glanced at the people with her—two women and a man, all older—and decided that they were definitely strangers.

'That blonde girl over there—she seems to know you,' I said to Nick, and winced as his fingers dug into the flesh of my arm.

He made a vague gesture towards the girl with his other arm and she waved in response. Then he hurried me away, or at least I felt as though I were being hurried. He made no attempt to comment on my remark.

We reached Piccadilly Circus and quite suddenly I remembered who the girl was.

'No wonder that girl knew you, Nick.' I looked up at him as we waited for the lights to change so we could cross a busy one-way street. 'She's a sister at Northleigh, isn't she?'

'Yes. On Nightingale Ward.'

'The women's counterpart of Fleming. What's her name? I ought to know it but I seem to have forgotten. Prunella—she's my friend on Nightingale—I mean, she *was* on Nightingale but she's going to another ward now, just like me——' I took a deep breath and abandoned that sentence. 'Prunella always refers to her just as Sister.'

'She's Sister Roberts.' The lights changed and Nick steered me across the road. 'I rather think you shouldn't have had that third glass of wine,

Kate. Do you feel all right?'

'Oh yes, thanks.' I broke off to giggle. 'It's only that I don't seem to be able to think very clearly.'

'It'll soon wear off if we walk a bit further.' His grip on my arm tightened.

'I don't really care whether it does or not,' I said dreamily. 'I'm having such a smashing time—nothing else seems to matter.'

It was certianly true—at that moment—that I'd rather be walking through the West End with Nick than at home in Glendale.

Soon after that we picked up a cruising taxi and my sobering up process continued when Nick sat in his own corner in silence and stared out of the window. I felt as if he'd retreated from me into a different world.

He did kiss me goodnight when we reached the flat, but when I would have lingered in the sitting room he pushed me gently away.

'Time we both went to bed, Kate.'

I fell asleep at once, in spite of my unfamiliar surroundings and slept late in the morning. I'd imagined myself getting Nick's breakfast but he'd already gone without disturbing me, and I ate a solitary meal and wondered what to do with the day.

A walk seemed to be the answer and I went out into a sparkling morning with frost still outlining the small amount of vegetation visible. Keeping well away from the hospital, I explored the neighbourhood and then decided to visit the Tower of London. This filled up the time pretty well, and when I returned to the flat there wasn't very long to wait before I could hope for Nick's homecoming.

He was in good time tonight and we went to the theatre. The show was out of this world and I was enthralled. Nick enjoyed it too and we arrived back at the flat in a happy mood, but once more he didn't seem inclined to sit talking by the fire.

The third day dragged horribly and I kept thinking about Glendale and wishing that, by some magic, I could spend the days there and the evenings with Nick. We had made no plans for this particular evening, which was just as well as he was very late and consequently disinclined to go out.

After we had eaten we watched television for a while and then, since there was nothing more that interested us, Nick switched off and came to sit down again. Only this time he sat much closer to me, so close in fact that he was able easily to slide his arm round my shoulders.

We were silent for a few minutes and then he said suddenly, 'Your parents wouldn't approve of the present situation. You realise that, I suppose?'

'Y-yes, but it's ridiculous.' I raised my head from his shoulder. 'They ought to know I was all right with you.'

'There's no "ought" about it, Kate, and I must say I think you're very trusting yourself. How do you know I won't suddenly snatch you up and carry you off to my room and make love to you?'

My heartbeats had quickened considerably. Was that what I really wanted? I didn't know and I felt confused and a little frightened.

'You—you said I could trust you,' I reminded him.

'So I did, but I'm only human, love, and you're a very attractive little person now you've lost your puppy fat.'

I was pleased that he found me attractive and once again we sat in silence. Then Nick leapt to his feet so abruptly that I fell sideways on the settee. He went straight across to the drinks table and poured himself a stiff whisky. I could see that his hand was trembling, and as I gazed at him apprehensively he swung round and faced me.

'For God's sake, Kate, are you really as naïve as you appear to be? I've admitted that you attract me, but I'm not in love with you and I do not want—repeat *not*—to show you any deeper signs of my affection than I've done already.'

I was appalled as I listened. Did he *really* think I'd been deliberately tempting him?

Perhaps I had, without realising it. Perhaps I really was as young and naïve as he seemed to think.

'I wish I knew which you are,' Nick went storming on, his eyes smouldering and his nostrils dilating with rage. 'A scheming hussy or a damned little fool! You must be one or the other.'

'I'm not scheming.' I was stung into defending myself. 'I'm just very fond of you and—and it seemed natural to show it.'

'Are you in love with me?' he demanded.

I was so long in finding an answer that he added impatiently, 'Are you? I want the truth, Kate.'

I decided to be completely honest. 'Sometimes I've thought I was, but I think—now—the answer is "no".'

'That's a relief, anyway.' Nick said, speaking much more calmly. 'The last thing I want is to hurt you.'

Because his sudden outburst of temper—so unlike him—had upset me badly, I tried to be flippant. 'Thank you for those few kind words. I suppose you don't mind if I continue to be just slightly fond of you, the way I always have been?'

'It's more than I deserve,' Nick said quietly. 'One of these days you'll understand what I mean.'

CHAPTER NINE

I CRIED a little when I got to bed that night, but perhaps it was only because a fantasy had come to an end. As my tears dried I began to worry about the last day of my holiday, and more particularly the last evening. If Nick asked me to go out with him it wouldn't be the same, and most certainly I didn't want to stay in.

In the morning I was glad because he'd left the flat before I was awake. I decided to get through the day somehow and let the evening take care of itself.

Once more my salvation lay in walking, and I went a very long way by the river, following the Embankment as much as possible. The Thames was looking beautiful in spite of its muddy colour and there was plenty of activity to watch. After a brief visit to a crowded snack bar, I returned by the same route.

I'd almost reached the neighbourhood of Nick's flat when I noticed a young man leaning on the parapet and staring at the water. His fair hair shone in the afternoon sunlight but I couldn't see his face. Nevertheless there was something about him which made me convinced that I knew him.

Suddenly he straightened up and turned away from the river. And I saw that it was Jeremy.

My first thought was that he mustn't see me. I came to an abrupt halt and looked desperately round for a way of escape, but there didn't seem to be any. The only possibility was to turn right about and go back the way I had come.

It was too late. Even as I started to swing round Jeremy looked straight at me.

I saw the astonishment in his face and paused. At all costs I mustn't appear to be trying to avoid him.

'Kate!' He came rapidly to meet me. 'I was just thinking about you—imagining how glorious it must be at Glendale just now. But what are you doing here? I thought you weren't due back until tomorrow.'

I've never been much good at lying on the spur of the moment. If I've got to tell an untruth I need to learn it by heart. Only that way can I give a convincing performance. There was certainly no time for that sort of thing now, and it seemed to me that I should stick as close to the truth as possible.

'I didn't go home after all,' I explained. 'My nieces are ill and it's probably infectious, and as they live in the same house——'

'That *was* bad luck!' Jeremy's voice was warmly sympathetic. Unconsciously he made the next bit easy for me. 'So you had to stay at the Nurses' Home? I wish I'd known—we might have fixed something up. What on earth have you been doing with yourself?'

'Exploring London mostly. I went to the Tower, and this morning I've walked miles along by the river.'

'But it must have been very dull on your own.' He was looking at me intently, his eyes very searching.

'Not too bad,' I assured him lightly.

A police launch was coming up the river, travelling at speed, and we both turned to watch it for a moment. Then Jeremy spoke again.

'Were you on your way back to the hospital? We might as well walk along together.'

That really put me in a spot. I didn't want to go anywhere near Northleigh until tomorrow.

'I'm in no hurry,' I said quickly. 'I thought I might explore a bit further in this direction.' I pointed ahead, the way I'd been walking when I first saw Jeremy leaning on the parapet.

But it wasn't going to be as simple as that. He immediately said he'd walk along with me.

'Is it your day off?' I asked. 'You don't normally have all this time for staring at the river.'

'It *should* be my day off, and in actual fact I've had the morning and afternoon free, but I've got to work this evening because the other houseman

135

has asked me to change with him. He's got a special date.' He glanced down at me. 'It's a damn nuisance, Kate, because if only I'd known you were at a loose end I might have taken you out for a meal. That is, if you're not doing anything else?'

I was so glad that Jeremy wasn't free, because of the awful complications which would occur if he took me out, that I answered much too cheerfully.

'No, I haven't arranged anything, but it doesn't matter. I expect I shall find something to do.'

'If we did have a date together,' Jeremy said rather gloomily, 'I expect we'd only argue all the time.'

'Perhaps. It seems to need some awful crisis—like being late back from Yorkshire, or climbing onto a roof-top—for us to get along without disagreeing.'

I'd meant the remark as a weak sort of joke but he took me seriously.

'Does it have to be that way, Kate? It does seem a pity.'

'I—I don't know.' I hardly knew what I was saying because we had now reached the point where our paths should have divided. It was only a short distance to Nick's block of flats and somehow I must contrive to leave Jeremy to continue towards Northleigh by himself.

To invent some shopping seemed the only possibility, and I came to a sudden halt.

'I'll have to leave you here. I've got one or two things to get at those shops round the corner. Be seeing you!'

Jeremy had halted too. 'Can't I come with you and carry your purchases for you?'

'Goodness—no! I'm not buying anything heavy, and I hate anybody waiting for me when I'm shopping.'

I waved my hand cheerfully and ran across the road. Jeremy didn't have any option but to go on alone.

Just to make my mind more comfortable I went into a florist's and bought some flowers for the flat. I'd noticed that Nick never had any. And then I looked round cautiously to make quite sure Jeremy wasn't lurking anywhere spying on me before I dared to walk in the direction of the flat.

I didn't feel really safe until I was inside, and then all my worry over Jeremy seeing me immediately turned into my other worry about what sort of mood Nick would be in this evening.

It was still early and I took a long time over changing into my green skirt, which would do for either going out or staying in, and attending to my make-up and nails. I laid the table in case it was needed, watched television for a while, and turned the pages of a magazine.

By this time it was getting pretty late and I began to wonder if an emergency had cropped up, or maybe he was deliberately remaining at the hospital so as not to be alone with me for very long. He didn't have anything to fear, I told myself indignantly, not after the things he'd said to me last night.

Suddenly the phone started ringing.

I had leapt to answer it before it occurred to me that it might not be Nick. If it was anyone else, it would be far better to let the caller think the flat was empty. I put out my hand and then withdrew it but I still hesitated.

If I didn't answer, I'd never know whether it was Nick or not.

'You took your time!' he snapped when I at last lifted the receiver. 'Listen, Kate, I'm very sorry but I don't know when I shall be home. We're just going to start on our second emergency operation and I've no idea how long it will take. Don't feel you've got to wait up for me.'

A sharp click cut me off before I had time to say a word.

What was left of the evening stretched emptily ahead of me. Although I knew it was better this way, I still felt bored and lonely and I wandered disconsolately about, not bothering to get a proper meal. Eventually I decided to do my packing, and I changed into slacks and a sweater and got everything ready for the morning.

Nick returned at eleven o'clock, looking tired

and yet jubilant. He was carrying a parcel wrapped in newspaper.

'I got some fried chicken,' he said, unwrapping it and revealing a red-and-white carton. 'Like half of it, Kate? I bought plenty in case you were hungry.'

'Thanks.' I followed him into the kitchen. 'How did the op. go?'

'Very well, after rather a bad start. The bloke was pretty far gone but I think he'll be okay now.' He got out two plates and divided the food. 'There's no doubt about it—it's a supremely satisfactory experience to be the means of saving a life.'

'It must be. I'm glad you enjoyed yourself.'

I hadn't intended to sound sarcastic, but Nick frowned.

'I don't think *enjoyed* is quite the right word, but I expect you'll be feeling cheesed off after such a dull evening. I'm sorry it had to happen but——' He shrugged and left the sentence unfinished.

I knew what he meant and I was glad when he changed the subject.

'By the way, how are your nieces? Has it been confirmed that they have glandular fever?'

I said guiltily that I hadn't phoned to enquire. 'I didn't like to, somehow. Mum would have asked questions and I would have found it difficult to reply. She'd have been sure to sense I was hiding something.'

'You don't regret it, do you? Coming here, I mean.' He looked straight at me.

I hesitated, unsure of my answer. Finally I said, 'No, I don't. I've had a super time and I'll always be grateful.'

We left it like that, without explanations or post-mortems, but I think Nick knew as well as I did that in future our relationship would be different.

In the morning I crept into the Nurses' Home like an intruder, choosing a time when there was very little coming and going. Even the earliest possible train from North Yorkshire couldn't have got me back as soon as that.

I was dreading meeting Prunella in case she bombarded me with questions, but luckily she was much too interested in some fabulous male she'd met at a party to bother with interrogating me about Glendale.

'Are you going to see him again?' I asked.

'Perhaps. I don't know yet. Actually, I'm rather inclined to think it was one of those one-night stands.'

'I expect Mac would be glad to hear that,' I suggested.

'Mac? It's got nothing to do with him.' She flung me an impatient look and then disappeared into her wardrobe. Her voice continued, muffled by the folds of a glamorous evening dress. 'Any

140

girl who took a houseman seriously would need her head examining. For one thing they're always on the move, and for another they can't afford to tie themselves up permanently to anyone.'

I'd heard it all before and I didn't pay much attention. As soon as Prunella had finished unpacking, we went to the cafeteria to get some food. We lingered over it, chatting idly, and then returned to the Nurses' Home.

It was as we were crossing the hall that the Warden popped out of her office and called to me.

'I've been looking for you, Nurse Wilding. Just come here a minute, will you, dear?'

Just for one brief second it seemed to me that my deception must have been discovered, that she knew where I'd spent the last four days. But I rallied quickly as I realised she wouldn't have called me 'dear' if I'd been in trouble.

I said, 'Yes, Sister? What is it?'

'A message from the Night Superintendent has come over for you. You aren't going to Whittington after all because of a staff emergency in the sick bay. Apparently they're very short-handed there due to holidays and sickness and they urgently need a junior nurse.'

''The sick bay!' I stared at her in alarm. 'You mean I shall have to nurse other nurses and—and even Sisters? Doctors too?'

'There's no need to look so scared, Nurse.' She

smiled a little impatiently. 'They'll be no different from other patients—some easy to nurse and some difficult, and it will be splendid experience for you with all kinds of different cases, from flu to major operations. Did you have a good holiday, dear?'

Hardly waiting for my reply, she went chattily on. 'Don't forget that you *must* go to bed tomorrow, even though you're not at all sleepy. A really good rest is absolutely essential before your first night on duty.'

The following day I conscientiously tried to follow her instructions, but I hardly slept at all and the time seemed endless. I was glad when I was able to get up, put on my uniform and go across to the dining room to eat 'breakfast.'

In spite of the Warden's reassuring words I was nervous when I reported for duty in the sick bay. I tried to tell myself that I'd been chosen because of my outstanding nursing ability, but I was more inclined to think I'd been picked with a pin.

There were a dozen rooms, some single, some with two or three beds, and the Night Staff Nurse in charge quickly put me in the picture. We had four operation cases who needed watching, a doctor who had to have his blood pressure taken every half-hour, and another who had been admitted because he'd had a cardiac arrest. The larger rooms held an assortment of nurses, none of whom seemed particularly ill.

I discovered that there would be only three of us on duty, the other being a third year nurse, and when Staff was off having her midnight meal she and I would be all on our own.

'Nurse Gray is very competent,' Staff told me, seeing my expression, 'and you aren't really alone, you know. You have only to lift the phone to summon the Night Superintendent and/or the appropriate houseman on call.'

I said fervently, 'I hope there won't be an emergency on my first night.'

'If there is, Nurse, no doubt you'll remember all you've been taught,' she told me quietly.

As far as nursing went my luck was in. Nothing untoward occurred all night and my biggest worry was my increasing sleepiness.

The crisis which did occur was in my own private life and it was totally unexpected.

About eleven o'clock, after we'd settled most of the patients down for the night, Staff Nurse looked at her watch and made a little clicking sound of annoyance.

'Dr Bradford is very late making his last round tonight. I want him to authorise some stronger sleeping pills for the patient in no. 11. She hardly slept at all last night.'

It hadn't entered my head that Jeremy might visit the sick bay, which was stupid really because most of the teams had patients there. I hadn't, in

143

fact, realised that every night young doctors went round the entire hospital, visiting every ward to check on the conditions of their patients before they could go to bed themselves. And after that, of course, they were frequently called out for emergencies.

It was another fifteen minutes before Jeremy turned up.

'I'm sorry, Staff,' he said wearily. 'I know it's terribly late, but I've been held up everywhere. I don't suppose you're needing my attentions, but I couldn't miss out the sick bay.'

He looked absolutely dead on his feet and the shaded light from the desk cast black shadows on his face, turning his eyes into deep pits and drawing lines of exhaustion down both sides of his mouth.

Staff made a brisk request for the sleeping pills and then glanced at him in concern.

'I don't know when I've seen you look so tired, Doctor.' She turned to me. 'Take him along to the kitchen, Nurse Wilding, and make him some coffee. Otherwise he may fold up before he gets finished.'

'It doesn't matter——' Jeremy began hastily.

'Nonsense, Doctor—it *does* matter, and Nurse hasn't anything to do just now. Off you go.'

I sped off to put the kettle on, and when I turned round I found him slumped in a chair at the table.

'Are you often as late as this?' I asked, to break a silence which somehow wasn't very comfortable.

'Oh yes—it's quite usual.' He folded his arms and stared down at them.

'Any reason for being extra tired?' I prodded. 'You're not starting flu, I hope?'

'I never have flu.'

As I put coffee in his cup I gave an exasperated sigh, and suddenly Jeremy looked straight at me.

'You really want to know why I'm like this, Kate? Okay then, I'll tell you. But I'm warning you—you may not like it.' As I stared at him in astonishment, he went bitterly on. 'I was on call last night and dragged out of bed several times. Fair enough—I'm used to that. But the night before I didn't sleep at all.'

I waited for a moment and then asked, 'So what kept you awake?'

'Thoughts.' He was still looking at me but I couldn't read his expression. 'It was the night after we met by the river. Remember?'

'Y-yes.' I still couldn't think what he was on about but I felt nervous.

'There were two emergency operations that evening,' Jeremy continued. 'Before the second one started I involuntarily listened in to a phone conversation. It was the boss who made it, in the corridor outside the theatre ante-room. I didn't mean to listen, of course, but I happened to be standing just inside the open door, and those damn silly hoods over the phones don't really make for privacy.'

Now I understood. By a most unlucky chance he'd overheard the brief call Nick made to me explaining that he would be late home.

I said as coolly as I could manage, 'Well?'

'Good God, Kate—is that all you've got to say?' His voice had risen but he quickly controlled it. 'You spent your four days' leave with Nick Marston, didn't you? Very likely you never intended to go to Glendale at all, and the yarn about glandular fever was all eyewash.' And, with even greater bitterness, he added, 'Not that it matters.'

'It *does* matter! I don't make a habit of lying and it was all true about the children being ill.' Now *I* had to struggle to keep my voice down. 'I was terribly disappointed and Nick very kindly offered to have me to stay at his flat instead. After all, we *are* old friends. I was grateful and had no hesitation whatsoever about accepting. He gave me a wonderful time—took me out to dinner and the theatre——'

'I bet he did!' Jeremy interrupted. 'And what was your part in all this, Kate? You don't expect me to believe he did it all for nothing. I'm not that daft.'

I was so furious I nearly slapped him across the

face. I had actually raised my hand before I got a grip on myself.

'How dare you!' I almost spat the words at him. 'What do you take me for? I'm not in the habit of *paying* my male friends in that way when they take me out. I never would have believed you could be so insulting.'

Jeremy was obviously shaken by my anger. 'I'm not suggesting you make a habit of it,' he protested. 'But you've always said Nick was someone special in your life, and anyone overhearing that conversation would have taken it for granted that you and he were—were——'

'Go on—say it!' I snapped. 'Lovers is the word you're groping for, isn't it? I daresay most people would have come to that conclusion, but I thought you knew me better than that. We've seen a lot of each other, for various reasons, since I came to Northleigh.'

'That's why——' Jeremy broke off and ran his hands through his hair, making it wildly untidy. 'I mean, it was because I thought I knew you that I was so—appalled.'

I looked down at him scornfully. 'And it didn't occur to you to give me the benefit of the doubt?'

'No, not then. I was too upset. But now——'

'Now it doesn't matter,' I told him with icy calm. 'If you could believe I was at Nick's flat for any purpose except four days' holiday, then it's not much good expecting you to accept my explanation. In any case, I don't care whether you believe me or not.'

But as I poured his coffee, spilling it all over the table top, I knew quite definitely that I did care.

CHAPTER TEN

I COULDN'T get my conversation with Jeremy out of my mind. I alternately blazed with anger because of the way he'd jumped to the wrong conclusion, or sank into the depths of depression for exactly the same reason. At no time did I dare to ask myself why I minded so much.

Night duty continued to be fairly peaceful, with periods of extreme busy-ness and long spells of calm. And then one night we had an emergency to cope with.

I was returning from my one o'clock meal when I heard the phone ringing in the office. Nobody was about and so I answered it.

'We're sending you a suspected appendix case,' said a distant voice. 'It's Sister Roberts. She roused the Sister in the next flat, complaining of violent pain, and then collapsed. She'll be with you in a few minutes.'

I went rushing off to find the Night Staff Nurse

who briskly ordered me to prepare a bed in a vacant single room.

As I hastily collected sheets and blankets and set to work, I reflected thankfully that Sister Roberts had the reputation of being very nice and Prunella had liked her a lot. She shouldn't be too terrifying to nurse.

When she arrived she was in no state to make difficulties. I had seldom seen anyone look so ill. Her delicate skin had turned a greenish-white and glistened with sweat, and already her lovely blue eyes seemed sunken. The pale blonde hair which had been hanging round her face when Nick and I saw her in Piccadilly was now spread out over the pillow, making her look very young.

She had severe abdominal pain, her pulse was racing and her temperature had leapt up alarmingly. Staff Nurse frowned when I showed her my first entries on the chart.

'She looks like being a case for Mr Marston, Nurse, but I don't think it's necessary to get him to the hospital in the middle of the night. You'd better call one of his housemen, though.'

I checked to find out which of them was on call and it was, of course, Jeremy. I wished it could have been the other one, whom I scarcely knew.

At first he didn't answer the phone and then I heard a dazed and unintelligible mutter.

'You're wanted in the sick bay, Doctor,' I said

formally. 'One of the Sisters has been taken ill.'

'Okay—I'll be there.' He was suddenly wide awake.

He arrived in less than five minutes, wearing jeans and a sweater and with a faint fair stubble on his jawline. Staff took him along at once to the room where Sister Roberts lay alternately groaning and apologising for making such a fuss.

'This pain is absolute hell.' She clutched her abdomen and writhed on the bed. 'I'll never be unsympathetic to a patient again—never!'

I wasn't needed there and I went off to answer a light which was flashing from one of the other rooms. It was nothing at all serious. A male nurse had had a nightmare and required soothing, and I spent a few minutes with him, getting him settled down again.

When I emerged Jeremy and Staff Nurse were talking in the corridor. They were agreeing that Sister Roberts was an acute appendix case.

'How urgent do you think she is?' Staff asked.

Jeremy hesitated. 'I think she can safely be left till the morning.'

'That is my opinion too, Doctor. Mr Marston wouldn't want to be called out for anything less than a real emergency, and Sister Roberts has admitted she's had pain like this before, only not so violent.'

I felt very sorry for our new patient. We were in

and out of her room all night, doing what we could to alleviate her distress, and round about half-past six I fetched a bowl of water and helped her to wash.

By now she didn't seem to have the strength to do much for herself and as I sponged her smooth young body I didn't feel she was a Sister any more. She was just a patient who needed my care.

'Thank you, Nurse.' She smiled faintly. 'You managed that very nicely and your touch is remarkably gentle.'

I was delighted at her praise and asked how she felt now.

'A little better, actually. The pain seems to be easing.' A look of anxiety flashed into her eyes. 'I wouldn't have expected that, Nurse.'

I was puzzled because she didn't seem pleased and ventured to ask why.

'The pain last night was too bad to stop like that. I think you'd better tell Staff.'

I collected the washing things and carried them out of the room. On my way to the sluice I reported the change in Sister Roberts' condition.

'Oh dear!' Staff Nurse looked even more alarmed than the patient had done. 'That could be a very bad sign. You've worked on a surgical ward, haven't you, Nurse Wilding? You must know that it's possible the abscess has perforated. The improvement in the patient's condition is rapidly followed by a serious relapse.'

I gazed at her in alarm. 'Will Dr Bradford get into trouble for not calling Mr Marston last night?'

'I really can't say,' she told me curtly. 'Get on with your work, Nurse.'

I supposed she thought I was too young and inexperienced to be allowed to concern myself with such medical matters. Nevertheless, when I met Jeremy entering the ward soon after—presumably in response to a phone summons—I took it upon myself to put him in the picture.

'It certainly doesn't sound too good.' His voice was very grave and he went striding off down the corridor.

I don't know what was said in Sister Roberts' room because I was busy with the early morning routine, but very soon after Jeremy's arrival Staff Nurse went to the phone and rang up Nick.

He reached the sick bay amazingly speedily, snapped 'Which room?' at me as though he'd never seen me before and barely paused to hear my answer.

I said quickly, 'I'll show you,' and hurried before him. As I pushed the door wider and ushered him in, I saw Jeremy standing by the window while Staff Nurse remained at the bedside.

The patient seemed to be dozing quietly, but at the slight stir she opened her eyes and said faintly,

'Oh! They've sent for you——'

Nick went over and took her wrist in his clasp. He said nothing but his face was very grim. Not daring to stay any longer, I pulled the door to and slipped quietly away.

But afterwards I saw Nick and Jeremy in the corridor, standing talking near the office. As I passed I heard Nick say tautly,

'Why wasn't I called earlier? *Why*?'

My eyes flew to Jeremy's face. He was very pale but he answered with composure.

'I had to take a decision, sir, and I took it. It seemed to me at the time that it wasn't necessary to call you.'

Poor Jeremy, I thought as I hurried on my way—he couldn't do more than trust his own judgment and it was desperately bad luck that he'd been wrong.

We soon learnt that Sister Roberts was to have an immediate operation and I was sent along to get her ready. I fetched an operation gown, socks and cap and took them to her room.

She grimaced when she saw the ugly garments. 'I hoped I'd never have to wear those! I've had this grumbling appendix for some time but I kept it to myself, and it always settled down again.' For a moment her lovely shadowed eyes were full of fear. 'I'm a terrible coward where operations are concerned, Nurse. I don't even like working in the theatre.'

She was already looking considerably more ill than she had done earlier and I guessed that the poison was beginning to spread through her body. There was an unhealthy flush in her cheeks and her hands were blazing hot.

'If you've been having regular bouts of pain you'll be glad to get rid of your appendix,' I said gently.

Sister Roberts sighed. 'Oh yes, I certainly shall, but I was hoping to have the job done at my own convenience. We're terribly busy on the ward just now and I don't know who's going to take over. It's very worrying——' Her voice died away and she closed her eyes.

As I left the room I encountered Staff Nurse.

'The theatre trolley's just arriving, Nurse. Is Sister Roberts ready? She is? Good.' She hesitated and then added almost apologetically, 'I'm afraid I shall have to ask you to go with her, as I've got no one else to send. I can't spare Nurse Gray. It's getting near the time for you to go off duty, but you won't be delayed very long.'

I assured her that I didn't mind in the least. 'I was sent to the theatre several times when I was in Fleming, Staff, and I know what's required of me.'

It wasn't very much; just to keep an eye on the patient and offer comfort if needed.

As we entered the theatre block after a long and

154

complicated journey from the sick bay, I couldn't help thinking of that extraordinary afternoon when Jeremy and I had sat up on the roof with Kevin. Where was Kevin now? I would very much have liked to know how he was faring.

The anaesthetist was ready and waiting and Nick came in as soon as we arrived. All I could see of him was his eyes, watchful and anxious, as he came up to the trolley.

As though sensing his presence, Sister Roberts opened her own eyes and gave him a faint smile.

I thought I heard him say very softly, 'It's going to be all right.'

I watched her slip away into total unconsciousness and then left. Nick hadn't seemed aware of my presence and I guessed he was very worried about the patient.

Back at the Nurses' Home I tapped on Prunella's door to see if she would join me in the brisk walk we were supposed to take before going to bed. To my surprise she was in her nightie and cleaning her teeth at the washbasin.

'Aren't you coming out?' I asked.

'No, I'm not!' She turned round, still scrubbing and speaking indistinctly as a result. 'We had a hell of a night, with a death and two admissions and the other patients having crises all around. Besides, I'm not like you—I don't go so much for fresh air.'

'We had a bit of a drama last night too.' I told her about Sister Roberts.

'I do hope she's going to be okay.' Prunella sounded quite upset. 'She's an absolutely super Sister and a very nice person as well. I'm not surprised Nick Marston was furious with Jeremy for not sending for him in the night.'

'It was just bad luck that Jeremy made the wrong decision,' I protested. 'Anybody could have done it.'

'You're sure to stand up for him.' Prunella yawned hugely. 'Do go away, Kate. I just haven't got the strength for argument just now.'

I was tired enough to follow her bad example but my inborn love of outdoors drove me to walk as far as the river. I was liking London much better now that the weather was colder, though I'd missed the sparkling autumn we usually had in Yorkshire.

By the time I got back to the hospital I judged that the operation would be over. I longed to ring up the ward and find out how it had gone but I didn't dare. I would have to wait until tonight.

It didn't seem long, because I fell asleep the moment I got into bed. In no time at all I was being called to get up again and go on duty.

My first job in the sick bay was usually to prepare the bedtime drinks. This took some time with so many separate rooms, and everybody had to be asked beforehand what they preferred to have as their nightcap.

I was halfway round when I came to Sister Roberts' room. The door was ajar and I was halted by the murmur of voices. As I hesitated outside, not sure whether to intrude or not, I suddenly realised that the male voice speaking in low tender tones was familiar.

It belonged to Nick, and he was saying very softly, 'I couldn't possibly go home without saying goodnight to you. How are you feeling, darling?'

I stood frozen, my hand uplifted to knock. I knew I shouldn't be listening but I felt powerless to move away.

Sister Roberts said drowsily, 'It's so wonderful not to have any pain. Was the operation quite straightforward, Nick?'

'Yes, thank God! But I could kill that houseman of mine for daring to take such a risk with you.' His tone was low and savage.

'Don't be too hard on him, darling,' her voice came pleadingly. 'He's young and still very inexperienced. Besides, I think almost anyone would have made the same decision.'

'*I* wouldn't, Sandra.'

'But you're prejudiced, Nick dear. You've got to remember that and make allowances.'

His only reply was a mutter I didn't catch. I was ashamed to think I'd been standing there listening to a very private conversation and I moved hastily away. Sister Roberts wouldn't want to see me just then, not while Nick was there.

And he wouldn't want me barging in either—that was for sure!

My mind was in such a turmoil that I hardly listened when the next patient—an elderly doctor—made his request for Horlicks and he reprimanded me sharply.

'What's the matter with you, Nurse? You shouldn't be day-dreaming on night duty!'

I've always hated being deceived and I felt Nick had treated me badly in not trusting me with his secret. I had so very nearly fallen in love with him myself, I now realised only too plainly, and he had done nothing to prevent it. He'd even admitted that I attracted him—physically, at least—and that confession could very easily have sparked off a response in me which we would both have later regretted.

I guess it's always painful when someone you've adored and looked up to turns out to be not quite what you thought. Perhaps Nick had never been the marvellous person I admired so much.

And yet—it might be that I was being too hard on him. I thought of his numerous kindnesses towards myself and softened a little. I mustn't make too hasty a judgment, I decided—and I must *not* let myself continue to think about it while I was on duty!

That night Jeremy was nearly as late making his final visit as he'd been a few nights ago, when Staff Nurse told me to give him coffee. This time she didn't suggest it and I dared not offer him any myself, though I thought he looked as though he could do with it. I was very anxious to tell him that Sister Roberts—the person most concerned— was on his side in the matter of Nick not being summoned, but I didn't have any opportunity of speaking to him at all.

It was a stroke of luck to meet him in the morning after I'd had 'supper' and was taking advantage of fine weather to cross the grounds instead of going through the tunnel to the Nurses' Home.

He would have passed by with a vague gesture of greeting, but I caught his arm.

'Can you spare a minute? I've got something to tell you.'

His thick fair brows rose in surprise. 'I didn't think we were on speaking terms, Kate.'

For a moment I couldn't think what he meant, and then I recalled how angry I'd been with him over his assumption that Nick and I were lovers. How could I actually have forgotten?

'We're not really,' I told him, 'but this is important. Let's go into the garden.'

It wasn't really a garden, just a secluded corner near the tennis court, and on a cold November morning there was no one there but ourselves. A misty sun was struggling above the surrounding buildings and a robin perched on a bush was singing joyously.

'What's all this mystery then?' Jeremy asked, looking at me intently.

'No mystery. I just thought you'd like to know that I overheard Sister Roberts telling Nick that it wasn't your fault she nearly got left too long. Anybody would have made the same decision in view of her history of recurrent bouts of pain.' I stared anxiously up into his face. 'Does that make you feel any better?'

'She said that—she really said it?'

'Yes, of course. I was standing outside the door and I heard her quite clearly.'

Jeremy gave a long sigh of relief. 'I don't suppose it'll be the last mistake I shall make, but it's wonderful to know the patient isn't blaming me this time anyway.' And he added stiffly, 'I'm tremendously grateful to you for telling me, Kate, but I can't think why you bothered.'

'Neither can I,' I said shortly.

There was something else I wanted to tell Jeremy but I wasn't sure whether I ought to, since I had learnt it by eavesdropping. Eventually I decided to approach it cautiously.

'Did you know that Nick and Sandra Roberts were—friends?'

'They get on very well together.' He hesitated. 'Is that what you meant?'

'I meant a little more than that actually.' I didn't go into details. 'But I think it's a very private thing and they don't want it talked about.'

'I'm not in the habit of spreading gossip,' Jeremy pointed out indignantly.

'Do you have to be so prickly?' I paused to swallow my irritation and ploughed on. 'I only mentioned it because it explains why Nick was so angry with you.'

'It certainly does.' He seemed to make an effort towards friendliness. 'In fact, Kate, I think you've removed about two-thirds of the load on my mind regarding Sister Roberts. The rest will have to stay there until I get over the ignominy of having made a mistake. No doubt it's very good for my self-esteem.'

'Could be,' I agreed lightly.

Jeremy was studying me curiously and he said in a puzzled way, 'I must say you're putting a very good face on all this business. In my opinion Nick Marston has treated you disgustingly. Inviting you to his flat and—and——'

'And what?' I flung at him challengingly, daring him to be explicit.

But Jeremy turned away, staring out across the tennis court. And at that moment the bleeper in his breast pocket set up its plaintive cry.

'I'll have to go.' He swung round again. 'We must finish this conversation another time, Kate.'

'Oh no, we mustn't!' I was suddenly so angry I could scarcely speak. 'If you *still* believe there was anything wrong in my relationship with Nick, then I never want to see you again outside duty hours— *never*!'

And I fled away from him, across the car park and through various short cuts until I arrived, breathless and furious, at the Nurses' Home.

CHAPTER ELEVEN

PRUNELLA was in a better mood that morning and we went for a short walk together before going to bed. I was glad of her company because my own thoughts were so chaotic and I didn't want to dwell on them. I was angry and hurt because Nick hadn't taken me into his confidence, and I was quite absurdly upset because Jeremy apparently thought I was a liar.

'You haven't been listening to a word I've been saying,' Prunella complained.

I started guiltily and confessed that it was true. Instead of leaving my problems behind I'd been carrying them around with me.

'It's no good expecting me to be intelligent at

this hour of the morning after night duty. My brain feels like it was stuffed with sawdust.'

'Okay, let's go back. D'you know something, Kate? We're both free on Friday night and we'll be able to go to the disco.'

'Smashing!' I said sarcastically. 'That's just what I need right now.'

'I suppose that means your feet are killing you? You'll forget all about that when you hear the beat.'

But it wasn't my feet which were worrying me but the thought that Jeremy might be there.

In the meantime, I had another night to get through before I was off duty for a short spell. When I went on that evening I found that Sister Roberts had had a restless day and they were still rather worried about her.

Nick was there but I kept well away from her room, hoping we wouldn't meet. I had an uneasy feeling that I ought to tell him about my eaves-dropping, and when I thought of all the various occasions in the past when I'd poured out my thoughts and worries to him, I could hardly believe that I now didn't really want to talk to him at all.

My keeping away from Sister Roberts' room did me no good whatsoever. I was pushing a trolley of empty mugs along the corridor when I came face to face with him.

'Hullo, Kate!' He stopped and smiled. 'I don't seem to have seen much of you lately. How are things?'

'Okay, thanks.' I increased my speed slightly and the trolley rattled dangerously. As I reached the kitchen and turned into it I found Nick was still there.

'Do you like night duty?' he asked conversationally, leaning against the doorpost.

'Yes, I do, thanks, now I've got used to it.' I was surprised to make that discovery. 'For one thing, I don't feel nearly so junior as I did in Fleming. When there are only three nurses on duty the jobs get shared out quite differently.'

He seemed to be in no hurry to leave and it suddenly occurred to me I could hardly have a better opportunity than this to make my confession. Staff Nurse was busy in one of the more distant rooms and Nurse Gray was doing a late medicine round. With luck we'd be undisturbed for a few minutes.

'Is Sister Roberts feeling better tonight?' I asked, by way of leading up to it.

A worried look came into Nick's eyes and at once I began to feel sorry for him.

'We shan't know for sure until tomorrow that she's going to be all right,' he told me. 'There should be a great improvement in the morning.'

'Nick——' I turned round from the draining board where I'd been stacking mugs and faced him. 'I've got something to tell you. I—I found out the other night that you and Sister Roberts are in love. I had no idea you were in her room and I was just coming in when I heard your voice. I'm afraid I stood there—just for a second—and listened.'

He looked at me silently for a moment, and then he said quietly, 'That doesn't sound like you, Kate.'

'I didn't *mean* to eavesdrop, but I was so surprised that I didn't seem able to help myself. Why didn't you tell me, Nick? I would have kept your secret safe.'

'Oh yes, I'm sure I could have trusted you, but Sandra insisted that no one must know until my divorce came through. She felt she was the cause of my marriage breaking up, whereas she was, of course, only a part of it. I'm sorry, Kate—I expect you felt rather hurt, but it was unavoidable. I couldn't go against Sandra's wishes.'

'You must love her very much,' I said softly.

'Yes, I do. In fact, I did my best to persuade her to move into the flat and not wait for the divorce, but she wouldn't agree.' His lips twitched into a half smile. 'Did it never occur to you, Kate, to wonder why I so conveniently had the spare key in my pocket that time I came upon you all upset because you weren't going to Glendale?'

I shook my head. 'I never thought about it.'

165

'I'd had it specially cut for Sandra, but she was off duty when I went along to give it to her. So you got it instead—temporarily.'

I felt more puzzled than ever. 'But didn't she think it was extraordinary that you should invite me to stay? I suppose you told her?'

For the first time he didn't meet my eyes.

'As a matter of fact, no—not at first—chiefly because I didn't happen to get an opportunity. But after she saw us out together in the West End, I explained everything.'

'And she didn't mind?' I asked incredulously.

'Well, of course, I made a good case for myself and emphasized my long friendship with your family and how glad I was to repay some of the hospitality I'd had in the past. Sandra quite understood after that.'

His slight embarrassment had vanished; he was once more very much in command of the situation—a man whose professional life must give him cause for great satisfaction, and whose private life would soon recover from the slight setback it had received when his marriage turned out badly.

But for me the old magic had entirely gone. As I studied him coolly I noticed for the first time that he was looking older. There were tiny creases at the corners of his eyes and his hairline had ever so slightly receded. Hitherto my adoration had blinded me to these telltale signs; now I saw them

166

rather too plainly.

I felt very sad because I'd lost my idol and there was absolutely nothing to take his place.

'I mustn't stand here talking to you, Nick. I've got to wash these mugs and put them away.' I turned back to the sink and ran hot water noisily, and when I glanced over my shoulder a moment later I was alone.

Soon after that Staff Nurse sent me round the sick bay to settle down all those patients who weren't waiting for a late visit from a doctor. This was a job I enjoyed as it gave me a chance to talk to those who felt in the mood for conversation.

Dr Graham, the middle-aged man who had told me off for day-dreaming, was feeling much more relaxed tonight. I knew from the report that he'd had a restful day and I asked him if he was likely to be discharged soon.

'They won't hear of it yet.' He plucked at the bedspread with long thin fingers. 'I feel such a fraud lying here doing nothing.'

'You should know better than I do that a good long rest is essential, Doctor,' I reminded him. 'It's not really very long since your heart attack, and I expect if they let you go home you'd only want to start work again.'

He sighed. 'You're right there, Nurse. I suppose I must be patient. It's not actually as difficult as you might think, because I do feel quite extraordinarily tired.'

I picked up a photograph from the locker. 'Are these your grandchildren? You must be very proud of them.'

He took it from my hand. 'My daughter's children—and a lively trio they are, too. The eldest is the one on the pony and the two little girls——'

There was a crash as the framed photograph dropped from his hand and fell to the floor. Dr Graham collapsed against his pillows, his mouth still open and his sentence unfinished.

For one terrible moment I thought he was dead.

I've never moved so fast in my life, though I was scarcely aware of conscious thought. Over and over again I'd had it drilled into me what I must do on such an occasion, and by some miracle I was able to act automatically, *without* thinking.

I leapt to the bedhead and pressed the bell with one hand while with the other I dragged out all the pillows and flung them on the chair. I checked the carotid artery and found no sign of life. Summoning all my strength I thrust my fist into the patient's diaphragm.

How long was it since I'd rung the alarm bell? It seemed an eternity as I pressed with both hands on the lifeless chest and waited for help.

It couldn't have been more than two or three seconds before help came. Strong hands came over mine and as I moved back Jeremy's voice said urgently, 'Mouth-to-mouth, Kate—alternately with me.'

I didn't know how he came to be there—Dr Graham wasn't his patient—and afterwards I concluded that he'd just been passing the door when the light flashed on and the bell rang like fury. At the time all I cared about was that he'd come and the responsibility was no longer entirely mine.

I took a deep breath and did as I was told. Vaguely I was aware of others in the room behind us, more and more people, so it seemed, but before I was really conscious of the terrific activity Staff Nurse had taken over from me.

I went to stand against the wall, panting and a little dizzy, keeping out of the way of oxygen cylinders and the cardiac team who had arrived at the run.

Suddenly Dr Graham gave a sort of groan and began to breathe again.

Jeremy stood back, and the team took over completely, and I heard Staff say quietly, 'Congratulations, Dr Bradford. You've just saved a life.' Turning to me, she added, 'You did very well indeed, Nurse Wilding. You could so easily have lost your head.'

I was thrilled at her praise, and when I looked at Jeremy to see how he was feeling I felt I'd never really seen him properly before. His whole face was alight, his eyes bluer than normal and shining with an inner glow, and I knew that I had glimpsed for the first time just what being a doctor meant to him.

'There are far too many people in this room,' Staff went on briskly. 'Go and get on with your work, Nurse.'

When I reached the corridor I found Jeremy had followed me. He still looked on top of the world, but by now I was feeling most peculiar and my legs were shaking uncontrollably.

'I—I think I shall have to sit down a minute,' I stammered.

He gave me a quick glance and slipped his hand under my arm. 'Is there an empty room anywhere near?'

'No. S, but——'

I'd been going to say that I didn't think I should make use of it and the kitchen would do perfectly well, but somehow I just couldn't be bothered and I let Jeremy steer me in and sit me down in an armchair.

'You'll be okay in a minute. It's a natural reaction.' His fingers were on my pulse.

'Sorry to be so silly,' I said feebly. 'Staff will have a fit if she finds us in here.'

'She's got her hands full at the moment.' He pushed the door until it was nearly shut. 'You're looking better already, Kate.'

'I've almost stopped shaking, thank goodness.' I straightened my drooping shoulders. 'I can't think what came over me. I didn't carry on like this when I climbed up on the roof.'

'And a good thing too!' He smiled, his eyes dancing. 'I was the one who came near to it. I've never been so scared in my life.'

'Yet you still went up there.' I looked at him thoughtfully. 'I suppose it was being a doctor that made you feel you must make the attempt.'

'Not entirely. I had—other reasons.'

I felt too lazy to ask what they were. If I hadn't been still so cold I would have enjoyed sitting there and doing nothing when I ought to have been working.

I began to rub my hands together and Jeremy came over and leaned against the edge of the bed.

'You're not making a very good job of that,' he said critically. 'Let me.'

He took both my hands in his own warm ones and began to massage them rhythmically, and I leaned back again and gave myself up to enjoyment of the moment.

'Did you always want to be a doctor?' I asked dreamily. 'Ever since you were quite young?'

'I reckon I was about twelve when I got the urge. After that I never gave up the idea, not even when my adopted parents were killed.' He paused in his rubbing and his eyes had an inward look. 'It's been quite different from how I imagined it, of course. I used to make up stories in which I saved people's lives—in accidents and on the operating table, all very dramatic, of course. I never even thought of the way we did it tonight.'

Suddenly he held my hands very tightly. 'D'you know, Kate—that was the first time I ever had to do heart massage for real. I'm so relieved that I managed it okay.'

We were silent as we thought about Dr Graham and how near he had come to death—at least I suppose Jeremy's thoughts were the same as my own. I couldn't be sure because he was looking at me rather strangely, almost as though he might be thinking about *me*.

There was a slight sound in the corridor and he dropped my hands as though they had burnt him. I leapt to my feet.

'I don't think we're safe in here any longer.' I was glad to find myself fully recovered. 'Thanks for looking after me, Jeremy.'

'You'd have soon felt better anyway.' He hesitated and continued in a very low voice. 'Actually I came in to tell you something and I still haven't got it said. It's what I was going to say when my bleeper sounded and you went dashing off in a temper.'

Abruptly I was transported from the warmth of

the unused room to the cold damp of the corner by the tennis court.

'Well? What was it, then?' I demanded in a whisper.

'I wanted you to know that I *do* believe your version of those four days at Nick Marston's flat. I can't think why I ever doubted you were telling the truth.' And he added very stiffly, staring over the top of my head, 'I would like to apologise.'

'That's big of you!' Frantically I whipped up my anger so he shouldn't see how pleased I was to be believed at last. 'What am I supposed to do now? Go down on my knees in gratitude because you've come off your high moral horse? If that's what you're expecting I'm afraid you're going to be disappointed!'

Jeremy was holding me firmly by the arms, so that I was a prisoner. He said softly, 'Oh, Kate— Kate—why must you be like that? I tried to put things right by apologising but——'

The door was flung suddenly open and Nurse Gray stood there. She stared at us in amazement.

'I couldn't think why the bedside light was on. What on earth are you two doing in here? Staff will do her nut if she discovers you.'

Jeremy said something under his breath and let his hands drop.

'For your information,' he said curtly, 'Kate had a bit of a reaction after all the fuss with Dr

Graham. I advised her to sit down for a few minutes.'

She gave a sort of snort and turned away. '*I'll* believe you but thousands wouldn't!'

When she'd gone, he looked down at me again. 'Is there no place in this hospital where a bloke can have a little private conversation without being disturbed?'

'Not when he's a houseman.' I slipped past him and reached the door. 'Sorry I lost my temper, Jeremy. It seems like it's becoming a habit where you're concerned. I shall have to watch it in future.'

I glanced cautiously up and down the corridor and then scurried away as fast as I could without actually running. Physically I felt fine now but mentally I was in a turmoil. It had been easy to refer casually to the future, but what could it possibly hold for Jeremy and me?

I thought of the three occasions when he had kissed me—so long ago—and I knew that I had yearned for him to do it again when we were together in room no. 5. I closed my eyes and imagined the hard warm pressure of his lips on mine, the feel of his lean body in close contact with my own.

Surely I wasn't falling in love with him?

No, of course I wasn't! There were times—far too many—when I didn't even *like* him. I was missing Nick, that's what was the matter with me, and probably jealous of Sandra Roberts. Could be I was the sort of girl who needed a man in her life.

If that was the case I'd better find somebody who didn't continually irritate me like Jeremy. And with this deliberately in view I went to the disco on Friday night with Prunella. Neither Jeremy nor Mac was there, and we got friendly with a couple of medics whom we'd never even seen before.

Unfortunately the one I got landed with was the sort who can't keep his hands off, and I got fed up and went back to the Nurses' Home before the disco finished. It hadn't really been a very successful evening.

Perhaps it would be better if I concentrated entirely on my work? I started taking a textbook on duty with me and tried to study it in the small hours, but by the time we started the morning rush I found I'd forgotten everything I'd read only a few hours before.

Patients came and went in the sick bay. Dr Graham had vanished to the Cardiac Unit but we heard he was making good progress. Sister Roberts recovered completely from the effects of her abscess having burst and went home to recuperate. I thought Nick was probably lonely during her absence, but I kept well out of his way.

He had no patients in our ward at the present time and so it was easy to avoid him. For the same reason, I saw nothing of Jeremy.

As my depression continued I told myself I was suffering from that well-known complaint called 'night nurses' blues.' Everything would be different when I was back on days, but that wouldn't be until January, after I'd been home for a short holiday.

One day Prunella reminded me that Christmas was getting very near.

CHAPTER TWELVE

'I SHALL hate not going home for Christmas,' I told Prunella.

'No doubt you always had an absolutely super time at Glendale!' She leaned forward to look in the mirror and carefully plucked a hair from her left eyebrow. 'I shan't mind not going home in the least, and everybody says you have a marvellous Christmas in hospital, even the patients. It's a pity we shall still be on nights, though.'

I did a little mental arithmetic. 'According to my calculations, Boxing Night is one of our nights off.'

'Really? Then we can be in the pantomime, Kate. They've been appealing for volunteers. I should think it might be quite amusing.'

'Which one are they doing?' I asked. I'd been living so much inside myself lately that I hadn't even realised there was a panto in the offing.

'Nothing recognisable,' Prunella said. 'It's written by the medics and contains bits from all the well-known ones and lots of grotty hospital jokes. They even break with tradition by having a male Prince.'

'What on earth for?'

'I should think it'd be almost impossible to find a nurse with good looks and good legs who could also dance and sing. It's easier for a man because he wouldn't have to pretend so much.'

'You *have* done your homework! I suppose you also know who's been chosen to play the Prince?'

'Of course I do.' Prunella turned round from the dressing table and faced me. 'Prepare for a shock, my child—it's Jeremy!'

'*Jeremy?*' I gasped and sat down rather suddenly. 'I don't believe it.'

'It's true. I always thought he was a dark horse, but I would never have expected to find him taking part in a pantomime.'

'Nor me.' I brooded over the information and couldn't decide whether it made me more or less interested in being involved myself. Not that I had any option, because Prunella announced that we would go along to a rehearsal on our next night off, and so that was what we did.

It was utter chaos and Jeremy wasn't even there, because he'd been bleeped just at the beginning. The authors kept changing the lines to suit requests from the players, and nobody knew what they were supposed to be doing at any given time. Prunella landed a tiny part and I found myself enrolled as a peasant girl.

After that we attended rehearsals as much as we could, somehow fitting them in with night duty. To everyone's amazement Jeremy made an absolutely super Prince once he'd managed to let himself go. Maybe he wasn't as handsome as might have been expected, but the way his fair hair fitted his head and just cleared his collar made him look marvellously picturesque, and he could sing just well enough to get by.

He didn't seem to notice me in the crowd scenes, but Prunella had a very short scene to play with him and she certainly made the most of it.

Christmas drew rapidly nearer and decorations began to appear in the wards. We had a giant Christmas tree at the entrance to the sick bay and fairy lights all down the corridor, even though as many of our patients as possible were being sent home.

Gradually the pantomime assumed some shape,

though nobody could imagine it ever being ready for a public performance on Boxing Night.

In spite of my unaccountable depression I enjoyed my first Christmas at Northleigh. On Christmas Eve there was a long procession of carol singers which wound its way through the hospital, starting with the children's ward and ending with the sick bay, where we had an impromptu party with mince pies and wine.

I was amazed to receive presents from our few patients in the morning, and also from the nurses. When I returned to the Nurses' Home I glanced automatically at the pigeon-holes where letters were put and found a large white envelope in mine with 'Nurse Kate Wilding' in an unfamiliar hand scrawled across it.

I tore it open and found another envelope inside with a Christmas card in it. This one was addressed to Dr Jeremy Bradford and he had scribbled over it, 'I received this from Kevin and thought you'd like to see it. Happy Christmas— Jeremy.'

For a moment I stood there, holding it in my hand and making no attempt to read what Kevin had written. I had received a beautiful and expensive card from Nick with an extravagant message in it, but I had so far had nothing from Jeremy and now he had only sent me a card from someone else.

Nevertheless, I was pleased to have news of Kevin. He wrote that he was feeling much better and the Medical Social Worker had found him a new home with a kindly middle-aged couple; there was even a job in the offing. He finished by saying how sorry he was to have caused so much trouble. 'Please tell the nurse I would have sent her a card too but I don't know her name.'

I was deeply touched that he'd remembered me and greatly cheered to learn that for him the future looked promising. When, later on, I happened to meet Jeremy when Prunella and I were touring the wards to admire the decorations, I thanked him for putting the card in my pigeon-hole.

'I knew you'd be interested,' was all he said.

'*You* don't sound exactly full of Christmas spirit!' Prunella commented.

'It's too early for that.' He glanced down at her and smiled, ignoring me. 'I shan't be able to relax until that damn pantomime is over. I must have been out of my mind to let myself in for it.'

'I wouldn't have thought it was your scene,' she agreed, and I added quickly, 'Neither would I.'

He was still giving all his attention to Prunella, and I wandered on down the ward. When she joined me she said she thought she'd managed to boost his morale a little by telling him how good he was in the part of the Prince.

'I thought Jeremy was supposed to be a friend

of yours, Kate.' She looked at me curiously. 'Just now I got the impression you couldn't have cared less about the way he was feeling.'

I turned my back and studied an outsize paper Father Christmas stuck on the wall. Had Jeremy received the same impression? It hardly seemed to matter.

'We were never all that friendly,' I said carelessly, 'and I don't see much of him now.'

We continued our tour and then went to our own wards for Christmas dinner. By this time I was moving in a haze of weariness and I was glad to crawl into bed about two o'clock and sleep away the few hours which remained before the pantomime.

In spite of a large number of unrehearsed incidents, it was a tremendous success and the audience applauded wildly. When I saw Jeremy in his costume for the first time my heart turned right over. He probably felt an utter fool in white satin breeches and a blue velvet coat, but he *looked* wonderful. He also managed to shed the last of his inhibitions and throw himself into the part. As the nurse playing opposite him was exceptionally pretty, perhaps it wasn't so difficult.

Afterwards there was a party in the hall where the discos were held. It went like a bomb right from the beginning. There was a lot to drink, since nearly everybody had brought a bottle of something, and there was plenty to eat too. We all talked and laughed and danced like crazy, and for a while I felt a wild kind of feverish enjoyment which I tried to persuade myself was happiness.

I had plenty to be happy about, I assured myself. I'd survived the loss of Nick with no more than a passing twinge of pain. I hadn't got into any trouble worth mentioning since I was late back from my grandmother's funeral, and on two occasions I'd acted promptly when faced with a sudden crisis. My career was certainly proceeding according to plan, and I'd had an absolutely super Christmas without once wishing myself at Glendale.

I had every reason to be happy!

It was when the pairing off began that the depression from which I'd been suffering hit me again like a physical blow. As I fended off the amatory attentions of a young doctor whose name I didn't even know, I wondered if maybe there was something wrong with me because I didn't fancy anybody around in that way; there was nobody with whom I wanted to dance cheek to cheek, or retire with into some dark corner.

And, like a fool, I believed I really felt like that—until in one blinding flash of revelation I knew it wasn't true.

Knowledge came out of the blue and I was temporarily stunned by it, so that the amorous houseman gave me up in despair and went off to find someone else. I hardly noticed he'd gone; I was too busy staring at Jeremy and Prunella.

I hadn't seen much of her during the party, but she had obviously been having a great time. Lots of the men there were attracted by her looks; she could have paired off with a dozen at least.

But the one she apparently wanted was Jeremy.

I saw her come up to him and fling her arms round his neck. His back was half turned towards me, and I couldn't see his face, but it seemed to me that he responded enthusiastically. He certainly put his arm round her and the sight was so painful to me that I literally flinched.

As I stood there looking at them I asked myself why I should mind so much because Jeremy was embracing my best friend, why I felt such a shattering surge of hatred towards Prunella.

And then I knew what had been the matter with me during the weeks before Christmas, and what was the matter with me now.

My feelings towards Jeremy had always been mixed, with actual dislike predominant at the beginning. Then there had been times when I liked him quite a lot, but always the pendulum kept swinging from one emotion to another until the muddle grew so great that I was sure of only one thing. I wasn't indifferent. I *minded* the way he treated me, and what he thought about me.

Out of all this confusion, love—true love—had grown quietly and unnoticed, but now it was so strong and vigorous that its stranglehold on my heart was an agony.

I was obsessed with an urgent need for flight. I *must* get away from the hot crowded room and out into the fresh cold air. When I was at Glendale I had always made for the moors if I was upset, and the cold uncaring streets of London would make a poor substitue, but they would have to do.

I turned and ran from the room, down the corridor to an outer door and through it into the night.

The air swept my hot face and I took a deep breath, slowing down to a rapid walk. The streets were surprisingly deserted and I assumed most people were indoors still enjoying their Christmas. Ignoring possible traffic hazards I plunged across the road and continued blindly into the tangle of narrow streets which lay beyond.

I had no coat, of course, and not even my hospital scarf to warm me, but I was unaware of the cold. As I hurried along I suppose I was instinctively making for the river, as being the only open space available to me in that part of the city.

I didn't get even a quarter of the way there.

I was walking down a dark street, my mind still totally occupied with the revelation I'd had at the party, when two youths came out of an alley on the other side of the road. I don't think I even noticed them until they shot across and barred my way.

'Where're you off to in such a hurry, darling?' one of them asked cheekily.

He had a narrow pointed face like a rat and long greasy hair, and his mate was similar but more heavily built. They both stretched out their arms, making a human barricade that effectively held me prisoner against the wall.

At first I was too angry to feel scared and I demanded sharply, 'What on earth d'you think you're doing? Let me go at once!'

'Plenty of time, love.' They were looking me up and down curiously. 'Where's your coat then? It's too cold for a nice girl like you to be out in a party dress.'

'She hasn't even got a handbag,' the larger one commented, and I smelt the beer on his breath.

'Sorry about that! I suppose you'd have snatched it if I had?' I asked sarcastically. 'Is that what you're after?'

'Nasty suspicious mind you've got, darling. We thought you might enjoy a little bit of fun, didn't we? There's plenty of quiet corners around here.'

Suddenly I was frightened and my fear was like an icy touch on my quivering flesh. I twisted round and tried to flee but they had me in an iron grip instantly and I was helpless.

I think I must have screamed, because one of them told me angrily to shut up, and then they both began dragging me towards the alley which had spewed them out into the street opposite me.

'Much better to come quietly,' I was advised. 'We don't want to hurt you—only have a little bit of fun like we said.'

I didn't believe them. I was sure they had knives hidden somewhere, and when I'd been raped I would be mutilated and murdered. I fought frantically, using every bit of my strength, kicking and struggling and even trying to bite.

If only someone would come, some ordinary sane person who didn't inhabit the dark world belonging to my captors, someone who would weigh in on my side and help me to win this terrible battle.

And then someone did come.

Above the sound of scuffling feet and panting I heard the blessed thud of footsteps behind me. A fist shot out and caught the rat-faced one a stinging blow on the side of his head.

'Get the hell out of here,' Jeremy flung at them furiously, both fists going like hammers, 'before I beat you both into pulp! Now—scram!'

'Be careful!' I whirled round and faced him. 'They may have knives.'

'Don't worry, Kate. They won't get near enough to use them.'

He looked so menacing standing there, tall and fighting fit, that after a moment's hesitation both youths turned and slunk away. We watched them vanish into the alleyway and heard the sound of rapidly receding steps.

'There wasn't much fight in them,' Jeremy said. 'Oh, Kate—thank God I was in time!' His voice shook.

I was suddenly aware that my legs were trembling and I felt sick. 'If you hadn't come——' I couldn't finish the sentence and I put both hands over my face as long terrible shudders shook my whole body. 'I—I was so afraid—it was horrible—horrible——'

Jeremy put his arm round me and drew me gently along in the direction of the hospital.

'I don't think we ought to hang about here, Kate, in case they've gone to get reinforcements.' His arm tightened. 'What on earth made you go dashing off like that?'

'I—I just wanted some fresh air.'

'Prunella thought you were feeling ill. She said you suddenly went white and shot outside, and we both followed you. We were just in time to see you whisking through the door. I sent her back to the party and came after you, but you set off at such a pace I almost lost you.'

His mention of Prunella had brought it all back to me. I'd been so pleased to see him that I'd

187

momentarily forgotten the reason for my flight. I tried to speak and couldn't because tears were choking me.

'I expect you're feeling the reaction,' Jeremy said gently. 'Poor Kate—it must have been an awful experience.' His voice was suddenly savage. 'I could have killed those two blokes with my bare hands!'

'Thank goodness you didn't try!' I struggled with the tears and gained a temporary victory. I even managed a feeble sort of laugh. 'It would have landed you in real trouble.'

'They might have called it justifiable homicide?' he suggested. His attempt at a laugh was no more successful than mine.

We reached the main road and paused on the kerb. His arm was still round me and I found it so wonderful that I wanted it to stay there for always.

But the hospital was only just across the way, with the party still going on, no doubt. I couldn't return to it as though nothing had happened, I just couldn't.

Inside the courtyard I halted and looked up at Jeremy. 'You go on without me. I'll take a short cut to the Nurses' Home.'

But he still held me firmly. 'I'm not letting you go haring off again. I'll come with you.'

As we altered direction it occurred to me that I hadn't really thanked him for coming to my rescue. Falteringly I tried to express my gratitude.

'I'll never forget how you came charging in and sent those two horrible creatures reeling back. It seemed like a miracle just when I most needed one.'

Jeremy didn't answer for a moment and then he said grimly, 'I don't think *I* shall ever forget how I felt when I saw what was happening. It would have been bad enough if it had been some other girl—but to see *you* in such danger—oh, Kate—Kate——' He came to an abrupt halt.

I stared up at him and my heart started thudding like crazy. 'I—I don't understand——'

'Don't you? I'm not surprised. I've been trying so desperately not to let you guess how I felt about you. You took a hard knock over Nick and I wanted you to get completely over it before I started plaguing you——' He stopped again.

I couldn't believe I was hearing him correctly, but in the midst of my confusion I had to put him right.

'I didn't take a hard knock. I was upset because he'd deceived me, but it didn't cause me any real pain.'

'Is that really true? Please, please, Kate, be honest with me,' Jeremy begged.

'Quite true,' I said steadily.

'Then there wasn't any real reason for hanging back except——'

'Except what?'

'I didn't think you particularly liked me. It wouldn't have been much good asking you to *love* me, would it?' he asked simply.

I caught my breath and gazed up into his face, and when I saw the look in his eyes it seemed to me—even though it was a cold dark night—that the whole world was suddenly full of stars.

'Not then it wouldn't.' I stood on tiptoe and wound my arms round his neck. 'But try asking me now, Jeremy dear!'

I don't know how long we stood there, in the shadow of the porter's lodge. Time had ceased to exist and I gave myself up entirely to the rapture of knowing that Jeremy loved me.

A long, long time later we came down to earth a little and started to make plans. One thing was for sure, I didn't want to give up nursing until I'd got my S.R.N.

'I never knew falling in love was part of the training,' Jeremy teased, 'and I certainly never had any intention of lumbering myself with a wife before I became a registrar.' He kissed me passionately. 'When can we get married, Kate? Soon?'

'Not till my second year, I'm afraid, because I shan't be allowed to live out before then,' I said regretfully, and suddenly remembered another problem. 'Oh, Jeremy, you'll be leaving Northleigh soon!'

'There are plenty of hospitals in London,' he assured me. 'If I can't get another houseman post at Northleigh, I'll find one not too far away. We'll manage, love. Nothing's going to keep us apart now we've found each other.'

It was getting colder and colder but we couldn't bear to go inside just yet. As Jeremy held me tightly to warm me, I began to think happily about the more distant future. He'd have a family now, for I knew he'd be welcomed into mine, and— looking ahead further still—if he still wanted to be a G.P. my father would probably be very glad to take an assistant so that he could relax a little as he grew older.

Christmas was over and in a few days a new year would be beginning. But for Jeremy and me it had already started.

Doctor Nurse Romances

Don't miss
September's
other story of love and romance amid the pressure
and emotion of medical life.

SURGEON IN CHARGE
(Winter of Change)
by Betty Neels

Mary Jane was over twenty-one, and a competent staff
nurse, so when she inherited a fortune she was furious
to find that she also had a guardian — the high-handed
Fabian van der Blocq. But what could she do about it
— or him?